SNAKES AND LADDERS

ADAM CROFT

First published in Great Britain in 2021.

This edition published in 2021 by Black Cannon Publishing.

ISBN: 978-1-912599-67-7

A CIP catalogue record for this book is available from the British Library.

Printed and bound in Great Britain by Clays Ltd, Elcograf S.p.A.

GET MORE OF MY BOOKS FREE!

To say thank you for buying this book, I'd like to invite you to my exclusive *VIP Club,* and give you some of my books and short stories for FREE.

You'll also be kept up to date with news on my latest books and given exclusive discounts on them.

To join the club, head to adamcroft.net/vip-club and two free books will be sent to you straight away! And the best thing is it won't cost you a penny — ever.

Adam Croft

For more information, visit my website: adamcroft.net

MORE BOOKS BY ADAM CROFT

RUTLAND CRIME SERIES

1. What Lies Beneath
2. On Borrowed Time
3. In Cold Blood

KNIGHT & CULVERHOUSE CRIME THRILLERS

1. Too Close for Comfort
2. Guilty as Sin
3. Jack Be Nimble
4. Rough Justice
5. In Too Deep
6. In The Name of the Father
7. With A Vengeance
8. Dead & Buried
9. In Too Deep
10. Snakes & Ladders

PSYCHOLOGICAL THRILLERS

- Her Last Tomorrow
- Only The Truth

- In Her Image
- Tell Me I'm Wrong
- The Perfect Lie
- Closer To You

KEMPSTON HARDWICK MYSTERIES

1. Exit Stage Left
2. The Westerlea House Mystery
3. Death Under the Sun
4. The Thirteenth Room
5. The Wrong Man

All titles are available to order from all good book shops.

Signed and personalised books available at adamcroft.net/shop

EBOOK-ONLY SHORT STORIES

- Gone
- The Harder They Fall
- Love You To Death
- The Defender

To find out more, visit adamcroft.net

For Maisie Daniels, there was nothing quite like the hit of cold, fresh morning air on the lungs. It always gave her a real high, and she loved the feel of her body aching as she pushed through the last couple of kilometres of her run.

It was running that'd made her realise she'd needed to leave Milo a few months earlier. She sometimes chuckled at the comparison, enjoying that early morning rush on her lungs and being left with an aching body. Then again, running was a lot healthier than smoking drugs and Milo kicking seven shades of shit out of her.

She'd seen so many people doing the 'new me' thing on Instagram, sharing their exercise routines, fun days out and pert little bodies after a particularly nasty break-up, and it was all so shallow and transparent. If their lives were so great and fulfilled, why did they feel the need to make such a point of it? Maisie half-remembered a quote from somewhere or other. *The lady doth protest too much.* No, she'd take much more pleasure from quietly and surreptitiously improving her life until that inevitable day when she'd pass Milo or one of his friends — and there weren't many — in the street. That would be so, so much sweeter. She knew that day could come at any time. It could be tomorrow, it could be today. And that pushed her on at every moment, made her work harder, run faster and push through that wall to get as fit as she possibly could.

She glanced at her watch to check her heart rate as she ran down Naismith Road, towards Mildenheath Woods. Not bad, but she could do with picking up the pace before she got onto uneven ground.

She pushed on further, feeling the burn in her legs and the cold air in her lungs, thinking only of that moment when she finally bumped into Milo and saw his face and how gutted he felt at having chosen a drug over her — the opposite choice to the one she'd made.

Before long, she was turning off the pavement and into Mildenheath Woods, the morning sun breaking through the clouds, beginning to take the chill off the edge of the air. After a minute or so, Maisie realised she'd been pushing it too far. The burn in her lungs was too intense, so she slowed down to a walk while she regained her breath.

Feeling her breathing starting to ease a little, she picked up the pace and walked further along the trail, feeling as though she might be ready to break into a jog again soon. Before she could, her eyes were drawn to a mound of disturbed earth, a few feet off the side of the trail. It seemed incongruous, the leaves having clearly been moved very recently. It didn't look like it'd been done by a fox or a badger, either; it was all too neat, too large.

She felt her heart skip a beat as the potential significance dawned on her. *Don't be silly, Maisie,* she told herself. Two years with Milo had made her automatically assume the worst in any situation. This didn't necessarily mean...

She had to find out. She pulled a chunk of bark loose from a nearby tree and started to dig, raking the loose, rich soil away. But as she removed the top layer of soil and revealed what was beneath, she quickly wished she hadn't.

Jack Culverhouse winced as the early morning light streamed in through his kitchen window. It was a far better wake-up tool than any coffee he'd ever tried, but he'd still be hitting the black stuff all the same. Over the past few weeks, his sleep had been worse than at any point he could remember, so even reaching a functioning state would be a bonus.

Functioning was as good as it got. Ever since his team's recent investigation into local organised crime, life and work had become purely functional. His world had been ripped apart by the revelation that Frank Vine, one of his longest-serving colleagues and a distinguished Detective Sergeant, had been feeding information to Gary McCann, a local criminal and Jack's arch-nemesis since becoming a detective.

Not only had Frank been feeding operational information to McCann, but he'd been actively losing evidence and information in an attempt to ensure McCann got off scot free — and it had worked. Jack had never quite understood how Gary McCann always managed to wriggle through the claws of justice, but the revelation of Frank's involvement had caused a few pennies to drop. Frank had never explicitly stated how long he'd been working for McCann, but Jack had his suspicions.

For Frank, there was no way out of this. His involvement had been clear, even if they were still unable to prove McCann's guilt. That was the most frustrating aspect for Jack in trying to nail his nemesis over the years — the way in which McCann managed to keep himself one step removed from any action, making it almost impossible to prove his involvement at any point. He had enough of a hold over his minions that plenty were willing to take the rap for him — and be paid handsomely for it. There'd even been rumours of those who'd refused suddenly finding themselves 'disappeared', but — yet again — evidence was thin on the ground to say the least.

But perhaps the most frustrating aspect for Jack was that Frank had clammed up, completely unwilling to talk or throw McCann under the bus. Despite having spent his whole career getting criminals locked up, Frank seemed hell bent on ruining his entire life's work by refusing to testify. Jack could see the logic: what was the point in Frank risking having his family harmed in return for a lesser sentence? He'd still be going to prison, and in any case his career and reputation had been ruined. With retirement around the corner and his health failing, there was a half-decent chance prison would finish him off either way, so it was understandable that he'd want to protect his family. But that wasn't enough for Jack.

To him, it was simple: if McCann was locked up, Frank's family would be safe anyway — as would everyone else in and around Mildenheath. They'd spent years trying to bring McCann to justice, only to be thwarted at every opportunity. Now, finally, they had their chance to nail him and it was one of his own detectives who held the key. However, with Frank having swallowed that metaphorical key followed by a lifetime's supply of metaphorical Immodium, it was now as good as useless.

To Jack, it was clear that McCann's grubby tentacles reached further than he could ever have imagined, and he felt more determined than ever to make sure the bastard rotted in a prison cell for the rest of his life. That determination, though — for now — was buried below a well of despair and utter despondency at recent events. Jack and the rest of the team at Mildenheath Police had faced the ultimate betrayal, and it was one they wouldn't recover from any time soon.

It had been a mild consolation to discover that McCann's wife, Imogen, had left him and moved abroad with the gardener, but it wasn't enough for Jack. Besides which, there were still heavy rumours that McCann had been responsible for the disappearance and death of his first wife years earlier.

Chrissie padded silently into the kitchen in her dressing gown and slippers. She'd been spending much more time at Jack's, and it was an unspoken truth that they were gradually heading towards her moving in permanently.

Their own relationship had been tricky, not through any sort of incompatibility, but sheer circumstance. Although Jack's daughter, Emily, claimed she was fine with her dad dating her headteacher, he also knew Emily took after him in managing to hide things. One thing she hadn't managed to hide, though, was her pregnancy.

'What's on your mind?' Chrissie asked, her voice almost a whisper, yet still making Jack jump.

'Nothing. Just looking at the garden.'

'You can't stand gardens. That's your "I'm looking out the window and thinking" pose.'

'As a matter of fact, I was thinking about getting rid of that rose bush and replacing it with a... something else.'

'It's meant to be good for you,' Chrissie said after a few moments.

'What is?'

'Gardening. They say it's good for the soul.'

'Bloody good job I haven't got one, then. I can keep my fingernails pristine.'

'It might help. Reconnecting with nature, taking a few moments to be at one.'

'Look, I appreciate your concern, but I don't think hugging a fucking tree's going to help much.'

Emily let out a laugh as she came into the kitchen and headed straight for the kettle. 'Not quite the line I was expecting to hear first this morning.'

'Yeah, well I like to keep everyone on their toes,' Jack replied.

'I find it quite relaxing,' Chrissie said.

'I'm not stopping you. Someone's got to dig that rose bush out.'

'Have you tried yoga?' Emily asked, not daring to look at her father for fear of descending into a fit of giggles.

Jack simply stared at her, causing Chrissie to pull her lower lip in and look down at the floor.

'So, what are your plans for the day, Em?' Chrissie asked.

'First antenatal class. Basically, I get to sit in a room and be patronised for an hour while a woman with no children tells me how to change a nappy.'

'Do you want me to come with you?'

Emily glanced up at her and considered this for a moment. 'Nah. It's alright. I'll be fine. Anyway, there's a yoga class going on in the next room and I wouldn't want Dad to start a fight.'

Chrissie returned a half-humoured smile, but it was laced with mutual concern for Jack. She nodded her head ever-so-slightly in his direction, nudging Emily to say something.

'Uh, Dad, I was wondering if maybe you might be able to show me a few things. The best way to do stuff, I mean.'

Jack turned away from the window for a moment to look at his daughter. 'Like what?'

'Well, like changing nappies and stuff. Getting them to sleep. All that.'

'It's probably all changed. They're meant to sleep on their fronts now, I think.'

'I think it's the other way round.'

Jack shrugged. 'I dunno. To be honest, by the time I got home from work the nappies were all done and you'd wriggled about in the cot so much you looked like you were doing a double pike.'

There were a few moments of silence before Emily spoke. 'I think you were a great dad,' she said. 'Still are, I mean.'

Jack dearly wanted to point out that it wasn't hard to look like a great parent when the other one was Helen, but he decided against it. He'd made his mind up soon after Emily came back into his life that one thing he'd never do is badmouth her mum. Helen was more than capable of digging herself into her own problems, without Jack helping and running the risk of slamming his shovel into an unexploded bomb.

Before Jack could think of a response, the ringing of his phone jolted him into the here and now. He listened as his colleague on the other end of the phone gave him the news, then tensed his jaw and grabbed his car keys.

3

Wendy felt her stomach rumble as she turned into the car park of Mildenheath Police Station, and quietly told herself she'd run across the road to the corner shop and grab herself something once she'd clocked in. Over-sleeping wasn't something she did often, even in the fog of confusion caused by ever-changing shift patterns and digital alarms, but she hoped she'd get away with it just this once.

She'd completely forgotten about the major roadworks in the town centre, only realising once she was in stationary traffic and a few yards past the last turning which'd allow her to take an alternative route.

She didn't curse her forgetfulness too much, though; her mind had been elsewhere, and for the first time in a long time the reasons were positive. She and Xav had settled down well together since he'd moved in, and she was feeling content in her role at work.

She'd recently made the decision, after much deliberation, to put in for her inspector's exams, having come to the realisation that she could indeed have a fruitful home life as well as a successful, forward-thinking career. It had taken her some time to realise that, and it was only after recognising that she'd been afraid of outranking her late father that she managed to come to terms with it and make the decision to move forward.

The whole team had been knocked for six by the revelations about Frank Vine, and Wendy had briefly wondered whether it was all worth it. The pursuit of justice seemed somewhat futile when one of their own team had been actively working against them and feeding information to a criminal gang, and she'd had a momentary existential wobble as a result. But it'd been Xav who'd focused her mind and allowed her to put things into perspective.

He'd reminded her that she had to look at the positives: there'd been a bad apple in the basket, and it'd been discovered and removed. They didn't know how long Frank had been corrupt, but they could be certain things hadn't got worse at all; they'd actually got better as a result of scraping out the rot.

Besides which, the team at Mildenheath CID had been fighting for its existence for years. With the rest of CID organised at a county level and — in the case of major crimes — often at a regional one, maintaining the town's own satellite CID unit had been something of an anachronism. County headquarters at Milton House had been trying to bring Mildenheath's resources under its banner for as long as Wendy could remember. The county's first politically-elected Police and Crime Commissioner, Martin Cummings, had been a keen proponent of merging services, but had been forced out of his job after it was discovered he'd been merging himself with the services of trafficked rent boys.

The election of Penny Andrews to succeed him had looked to be the final nail in the coffin for Mildenheath CID, but their success rate combined with the rooting out of Frank Vine had given them breathing space — and the express support of the new Police and Crime Commissioner.

For Wendy, it sometimes felt as though going into work gave her respite. When she was at home, she spent more time overthinking things, causing herself undue stress and anxiety. Even though most of those problems were caused by work, being here gave her focus and allowed her to concentrate on the task in hand rather than worrying about things that'd either already happened and couldn't be changed, or which might never happen anyway.

She parked her car in an empty space, and looked up at the brick building — an icon of seventies architecture, if those two words could ever go hand-in-hand. As she switched off her engine, her phone rang on the seat beside her. She glanced over and saw Jack Culverhouse's name on the screen.

'Hi,' she said, answering it. 'Yeah, I know, I know. I'm late. Sorry, it's this new phone and the bloody stupid alarm. I'm literally in the car park now. I thought I was going to make it, but those sodding roadworks on the High Street held me up.'

'Right, well you'll have to go through them again now, won't you? I need you over at Mildenheath Woods. There's a body.'

4

Jack stepped out of his car and onto the gravel surface of one of the car parks at Mildenheath Woods. It was a chilly morning, although it was meant to warm up later. Then again, the forecasts had been saying that for more than a week, and it hadn't turned out to be right yet.

A uniformed officer greeted him and led him into the woods towards the site where the body had been discovered, although Jack could've quite easily worked it out for himself by heading towards the sound of voices and the bright lights of the assembling scenes of crime team. When he got there, he noticed Dr Janet Grey, the pathologist, had already arrived. Although Dr Grey served a much wider area than just Mildenheath, the fact that she lived locally meant she was often on the scene quickly — and occasionally even before the senior investigating officer had arrived.

'You're even earlier than I expected, Jack,' she said, smiling.

'Yeah, I was out dogging in the other car park.'

Although gallows humour was a staple part of policing at the best of times, Jack had always enjoyed a good relationship with Dr Grey, and secretly quite enjoyed their comments towards each other. In reality, Mildenheath Woods was closer to Jack's house than the police station was, so it had been merely fortunate that he'd not yet left for work when the call had come in.

The officers on the scene had created an outer cordon around the perimeter of the woods itself, with the inner cordon being much smaller. Jack kept his distance, although he was still more than able to see the scene in front of him.

The body lay on its side in the mud and dirt. Although the victim was heavily covered in blood and soil, it was still clearly identifiable as a young male.

'Are his hands tied behind his back?' Jack asked, looking more closely.

'Cable-tied,' Dr Grey replied. 'Pretty tight, too. Whoever did it certainly didn't want him getting out of it. There are one or two other oddities, too. Obviously the whole body's pretty dirty from being buried in a shallow grave, but the knees are particularly muddy and damp. The dirt looks pretty ingrained in the trousers there, too, rather than having just been thrown loosely on top. That leads me towards thinking he might've been pushed to his knees at some point, or at least certainly knelt down heavily of his own accord.

'Christ. Looks like a mafia-style assassination.'

Dr Grey shrugged. 'Not for me to decide. I can only

give you the facts. But if I was in your shoes, I imagine I'd probably be thinking much along the same lines.'

'Definitely murder?' Jack asked.

Dr Grey smiled and wagged her finger. 'You won't catch me out that easily. All these years and you still try to box me into a corner. It's the detective in you, Jack.'

'If you were in my shoes, then?'

'I wouldn't be. With the number of pine trees in here, the mud'll be pretty acidic. I wouldn't want to be walking through here in shoes as cheap as those.'

'These are Hush Puppies,' Jack said, looking affronted.

'I know. But to answer your question as it was intended, all I can do is point you toward the facts. Our mutual friend was likely on his knees in the mud for some time, hands bound behind his back with cable ties, heavily beaten, considering some of the early bruising here. Judging by the amount of blood and the deep neck wounds, I imagine the slitting of his throat is what caused his death. I mean, I don't think it's beyond the bounds of my responsibilities to assume he probably didn't do that to himself. Not with his hands in that position, anyway. Oh, and there's some residue on his left cheek and upper lip, which looks like a sort of glue. It looks like some of his facial hairs — not that there are many — have been ripped out at the root. If I was a betting woman, I'd say there was probably some fairly hefty tape over his mouth at one point, which was subsequently torn off and discarded.'

Jack thought about this for a few moments. It seemed quite clear to him this was likely to be premeditated murder. For someone to have prepared tape and cable ties, lured or brought their victim out into the woods and then beaten him to his death required a certain degree of planning and foresight. Although the ramifications of that were much bigger from a criminal standpoint, it often made investigations much easier. For someone to go to that extent of planning, and to inflict that level of damage required them to really want the victim dead. Those sorts of nemeses tended to be quite easily identifiable once the victim's life was explored and uncovered. In many ways, the scarier cases were ones where the victim encountered a malevolent stranger on the way home, or got into an argument with a random person outside a bar. Fortunately, though, stranger murders were rare, and it seemed to Jack as though this case was likely to be one where the killer was known to the victim. 'Any ID on our man?' Jack asked.

'None whatsoever. No phone, no wallet, nothing.'

Jack nodded slowly as he considered that perhaps this investigation wouldn't go quite as smoothly as he'd anticipated.

'You're late,' Jack barked as Wendy walked towards him, twigs and bark crunching and snapping under her feet.

'I know. I told you I would be. What's the SP?'

Jack walked towards her and gestured for her to follow him back towards the car park. 'Young male, early twenties at best. Cause of death, deep knife wounds to the throat. Likely bled out, but evidence he'd been beaten too. Hands tied behind his back with cable ties, evidence he'd had tape over his mouth at one point, mud on his knees. Dr Death thinks he spent a lot of time on his knees. And yes, I already thought of the dogging joke, but I blew my load too early on that one. So to speak.'

'I'm guessing this is one of those "should've been there" moments?'

'Something like that.'

'Doesn't sound good, though. From the way you've described it, it sounds like an assassination.'

'Exactly what I said. Ten quid says drugs are involved

somewhere along the line. Either that or some satanic death cult.'

Wendy thought about this for a moment, but there was something else on her mind. 'You seem… I dunno.'

'What?'

'I dunno. Brighter.'

'Brighter? Than what?'

'Than you have been.'

'Lovely. Thanks. And no, I'm not "brighter". I've got the bit between my teeth because we've got a job on. It's what we're paid to do.'

Wendy nodded. 'So are you still… you know.'

'No. No, I don't know.'

'Well, I mean, I just wanted to check in with how you're doing. I know recently things have been tough. For everyone, I mean. But I know it's been difficult for you in particular. And after the problems there've been in the past, I wanted to make sure you were in the right head-space for this. As a friend, I mean.'

Jack stopped walking and looked at her. 'I'm not your fucking friend, Knight.'

'I know. Doesn't stop me being yours, though. If it helps you reconcile it in your emotionless mind, just assume I'm concerned out of self-interest because I don't want the investigation to go down the pan and for us to all have to work from Milton House.'

'That ain't gonna happen,' he said, on the move again. 'If anything, we've got even more chance of getting results now we haven't got a fucking rat in the office.'

'We had good results even before that.'

'There we are, then. No need to worry, is there,' Jack replied, more as a statement than a question.

'And how's Emily?' Wendy asked as they reached the car park.

'Yeah. Fine.'

'How far along is she?'

'Nearly twenty-eight weeks,' Jack replied. Wendy noticed a glimmer in his eye as he said this, before it was replaced with something altogether different.

'How are you all coping with it?' she asked.

Jack shrugged. 'Nothing much to cope with, is there? I mean, it's not like I'm the one carrying a baby around.'

'Well, no. Not physically, maybe. But there's a lot more to it than that. I can't imagine it's easy, considering.'

'What, at my age, you mean?' he answered with a wry smile.

'To be fair, you're practically a spring chicken in the grandfather world.'

'Mmmm. Gonna be more than that, though, ain't it?'

'The dad still not interested?'

Jack shook his head. 'No. I dunno whether that's a good thing or a bad thing. It is what it is, I guess. Not gonna be easy, but probably for the best.'

Wendy smiled with one corner of her mouth. 'Listen,' she said, 'if you ever want to talk about anything — Emily, home stuff, the whole Frank thing — whatever it is, I'm here, alright?'

Jack looked at her. 'I'm fine,' he said, before getting into his car. 'See you back at the office. Try and avoid the roadworks this time, yeah?'

Jack stood at the front of the major incident room and addressed his team, which was, of course, now one man short.

'Okay. This is the first briefing on Operation Artisan,' he said, complete with air quotes around the name that'd been generated by the police computer. This was, like many things, something for which Jack couldn't quite bring himself to muster up the tolerance. 'It concerns the murder of an as-of-yet unnamed male, in his late teens or early twenties. His body was discovered by a jogger in Mildenheath Woods early this morning. All we know at this stage is that he appears to have spent some time on his knees — no jokes, please, Steve,' he said, looking pointedly at DS Wing, 'and had his hands tied behind his back with cable ties. The official cause of death is yet to be determined, but it's likely to come back as showing he bled out due to the knife wounds to his neck. He'd been beaten badly around the head and body with an unknown blunt instrument, potentially something quite heavy like a crowbar or a tool of some sort. We'll get more information on that when it comes in. The only other piece of evidence we have so far is the presence of an adhesive around his mouth area, which Dr Grey reckons is from some heavy-duty tape, which was presumably placed over his mouth to silence him during the ordeal. That piece of tape hasn't been found, so we're looking at the presumption that the killer took it with them. Any questions?'

'What state was the body found in?' Ryan Mackenzie asked, chewing the end of her pencil.

'A pretty bloody shit one,' Jack replied. 'Buried in a shallow grave, covered with loose soil and leaves. There's evidence a shovel was used to dig it, but evidently our killer either didn't realise how much earth has to be shifted to bury a body, or he was too knackered from his little exertions a few minutes earlier. Ryan, while you're listening, can you look at missing persons and see if there's anyone on the list who matches the description? We'll keep eyes and ears on the ground, too, because if our boy hasn't been reported missing yet, it's likely he will be at some point. We've made frontline aware.

'We don't think there's CCTV covering the car park at the woods,' he continued, 'but Steve, can you get onto the council to double-check please? You and Debbie can pop down and have a wander about the residential roads that surround the woods, maybe see if anyone has CCTV on their house that might cover any other ways in. If our man's gone in and out with a shovel and some heavy tools, he'll either be blindingly obvious or in a car. Either way, it's a lead.'

'The shovel could've been used to beat him, too,' Debbie Weston offered.

'Possibly. I thought that, but the bruising and markings indicate it probably wasn't. They're still scouring the woods for anything that's been dumped, but nothing's been found yet. Our main priority at the moment is finding the knife. If that's got DNA evidence or fingerprints on it, or if we can trace it back to its owner, we're onto a winner. On the shovel, I doubt we'll find it. I don't think it's likely our killer will've taken the tape off the lad's mouth to hide that piece of evidence, then left his shovel up against a tree somewhere. We're working on the assumption we won't find it easily. I imagine this'll be one of those where things drip in over time, so we'll crack on with what we have and we'll update as and when we need to. Class adjourned.'

As Jack opened the door to his office, his phone began to ring. He leaned over the desk to pick it up, then listened as the officer on the other end gave him the message.

Jack wrote down the details on a piece of paper, then headed back out into the incident room. 'Okay,' he said, getting his team's attention. 'We've had a call come in from some concerned parents, saying their little darling didn't come home last night. They're not able to get hold of him and were panicking, so they phoned the police. It sounds like he matches the description of our victim, so we're going to head over and confirm. Knight, grab your coat. You're coming with me.'

7

Dale and Cleo Hulford's house didn't look like the home of a teenager who got themselves into drugs. Jack and Wendy knew from experience that stereotypes were there to be broken, but they each had a sense that all wasn't as it seemed as they parked up at the end of the driveway and looked around them.

'Nice street,' Wendy said.

'Well, yeah. What else did you think you were gonna get when you saw the words "Private Road" at the entrance?' Jack replied, getting out of the car.

They walked up the Hulfords' driveway and pressed the doorbell — an old-fashioned affair that sounded as if it was ringing bells throughout the house. A few moments later, a tall, lanky man in a chequered short-sleeve shirt and chinos answered the door.

'Mr Hulford? Jack Culverhouse and Wendy Knight, from Mildenheath Police. You called to say your son was missing?'

'Yes. Yes, come in,' Dale Hulford said, stepping to one side. 'I must admit, I didn't think they'd send two detectives out. I didn't think you took these things seriously until someone had been missing for a couple of days.'

'You'd be amazed how many people think that,' Jack replied, not wanting to give him false hope, nor write his son off as dead without confirming his identity.

'Would you like a tea? Coffee?' Dale asked, gesturing vaguely in the direction of the kitchen.

'We're fine, thanks,' Jack said, knowing from experience that hot drinks served at home visits tended to be comparable to the boiled piss that came out of the coffee dispenser at work.

They sat down in the living room, Jack and Wendy having been introduced to Dale's wife, Cleo. Although they knew they couldn't jump to conclusions based on appearances, the Hulfords didn't look like the parents of a young lad who got himself assassinated in the woods at night.

'So you mentioned that your son didn't come home last night,' Wendy said. 'Matt, isn't it?'

'Matthew, yes,' Cleo replied. 'We were expecting him to be in by ten or eleven, but he is back late sometimes. He usually sends us a text, but even then we don't tend to worry too much if he's a bit late. We've both been a bit under the weather, so we went to bed a bit earlier last night and just assumed he'd be back. I woke a couple of times in the night and he wasn't here, and Dale said to leave it until the morning in case he'd slept over at his friend's house.'

'Is that where he was?'

Cleo nodded. 'Connor French. They've been insepa-rable since junior school. Matthew goes over there quite often to play video games, and he's sometimes out late, but he's never stayed out all night before.'

'And did you try getting hold of him overnight?' Wendy asked.

'We texted him a couple of times and tried ringing,' Dale said, 'but it went straight to voicemail. We thought maybe his battery had run out, so we left it until the morning then we called Connor, but he said Matt left his last night and headed home. That was the last time anyone saw him.'

'And are there any other friends he might have gone to see?' Wendy asked. 'Anyone who's on the way home, other places he might've gone?'

Cleo shook her head. 'No. We've been racking our brains, but there really isn't anyone. Matthew's such a nice, quiet lad, but he doesn't really have many friends other than Connor. He's always been quite studious and did well at school. He's not really one for big groups of friends or anything like that. He and Connor always keep themselves to themselves.'

'And has he ever been in any trouble?'

'No, never. Not in the slightest. We're not that sort of family. That's why it's all so bizarre.'

'I can understand how worrying it must be,' Wendy said. 'And I can see how out-of-character it is for him. Do you have any photos of Matt which we could have, please? Just so we can circulate them internally and make sure officers are aware.'

'I've got a couple on my phone,' Dale said, taking it out of his shirt pocket and opening the leather flip cover. 'One moment... yes, here we go. This one was taken at my brother's fiftieth birthday party a couple of weeks ago. That's Matt there, on the far left.'

Dale passed the phone to Wendy, who zoomed in on the picture of Matt Hulford, before turning the phone to show it to Jack. Even though the body in the woods had been beaten and its throat had been cut, the face had been left relatively unscathed, and as far as Jack and Wendy were concerned, there was very little doubt now as to his identity.

Wendy looked up at Dale and Cleo Hulford and did her best to form the right words.

8

Frank sat on the hard bed of his prison cell and looked at the wall opposite. It was something he'd got used to doing, and which he found much more pleasant than many of the alternatives.

This wasn't where he belonged. He'd spent his whole life putting people in places like this, and he knew he wouldn't last five minutes if his fellow inmates knew who he was and why he was here.

So far, he'd managed to evade the truth by packaging up a series of lies. It was something he'd got quite good at, and was precisely why he'd ended up here in the first place. Mostly, though, he kept himself to himself.

It had been suggested that protection would be needed. Ex-cops tended not to fare well inside. But Frank had insisted against it, knowing this would 'out' him immediately, and that he couldn't be protected forever. Instead, he'd made up a cock and bull story about fraud and extortion in the wake of a business deal gone wrong.

It was clear he wasn't a killer or drug dealer, and it would at least explain why he seemed scared and withdrawn.

He didn't know if he was just being paranoid, but he could swear other inmates had started to give him the side-eye recently. He'd been careful to make sure he didn't know any of the other prisoners from his time in the police, having already been moved once after spotting a previous client in the first prison he was sent to.

He'd been tempted — sorely tempted — to end it all on more than one occasion. Not long after his arrest and charge, a fellow officer had even offered to help him out. But as much as that seemed like a welcome relief, there was no way Frank would ever do such a thing. It would mean that everything was a waste, whichever way he looked at it. His life would end on this extraordinary, shameful low. His career would've been wasted. Even those he'd wronged would've gone without justice. After everything that'd happened, Frank knew he absolutely needed to stay the course, and he had no intention of doing anything else.

A prison officer knocked on the open door and cocked his head. 'Yard time,' he said.

'I'm alright. Not feeling great.'

'You'll feel better for the fresh air.'

'I won't.'

The officer shuffled his weight onto his other foot. 'Mike?' he called over his shoulder, waiting for his colleague to appear. 'I'll let you handle this one,' he said to his colleague, before walking back along the landing.

'What's the matter, Frank?'

'Nothing. I just don't want to go outside. Why does that have to be a problem?'

'Feeling ill?' Mike asked. Over the course of the last few weeks, Frank had developed a good relationship with Mike. It had, of course, remained strictly professional, but he at least felt that Mike had his best interests at heart.

'Yeah.'

'You've been telling me you've been feeling ill every day for the past week. It's clearly not making you feel any better staying in here, is it? Now listen. I've got a responsibility to look after your health. That means getting outside, getting some sun on you and getting some fresh air.'

'Honestly. I'm fine,' Frank said.

Mike looked behind him, then stepped into the cell. 'Frank, I know you're not doing all that well in here. White-collar-crimers rarely do. But my job's to make sure there's no trouble and that everyone's welfare is taken into account. I know some of the guys in here can be intimidating, but I promise you, it's all bluff. They feel they've got to do it to feel safe. They don't trust us. They think they run the place. If their constant one-upping each other makes them feel safe, then so be it. But you and I know they're not the law, don't we?'

Frank's heart skipped a beat. He looked at Mike, wondering if there was more to his words than he let on, but Mike's eyes conveyed nothing but sincerity and kindness. He was amazed the guy hadn't been eaten alive in here, but he seemed to have a manner which yielded respect from even the most hardened of criminals.

'Yeah, I know. It's fine.'

'And the more you hide in here and close in on yourself, the more you'll make yourself a target for people like them. I'm not saying you need to stroll out of here like Charles Bronson, but hold your head up. Keep quiet by all means, but don't look like you're inviting a pasting. Come on. Let's get you up and outside.'

Frank looked at him.

'You'll be fine,' Mike said. 'I promise. We'll keep an eye on you.'

It had been a while since Frank had felt the sunshine on him. It felt good — he couldn't deny that. But he knew he'd never be able to truly relax in this place. The old saying went that there was only one thing worse than a copper, and that was a bent copper.

He looked around him, spotting Mike on the other side of the yard. Frank held his head up, trying to take his advice, not wanting to stand out like a sore thumb and invite hassle.

As he took in lungful after lungful of crisp morning air and felt the sun on his face, he noticed a group of three inmates walking towards him, almost a singular mass of grey sweatshirts and sweatpants. He could see from the looks in their eyes that they weren't here to discuss classical music.

'What you afraid of, fella?' one of the men said.

'Nothing. Why?' Frank replied.

"Cos you've been acting fucking weird ever since you got here. What you in for?'

'Fraud and extortion. I got done over on a business deal and should've backed down earlier. I didn't.'

The man nodded slowly. 'I guessed you're not exactly used to being inside.'

Frank didn't reply.

'What line of business was you in?' the man asked.

'Financial investments.' This was the stock answer Frank'd had up his sleeve ever since he knew he'd be spending time in prison. He was pretty sure he wasn't going to come across many city traders in here, and if he did they wouldn't be the ones asking him questions.

'What sort of investments?'

'Financial ones,' Frank replied, almost immediately regretting his sass, but at the same time hoping it might make him seem like less of a weak sap.

'You don't look like a financial guy to me.'

'Yeah, well they wouldn't let me wear my suit in here.'

'You ain't in for fraud and extortion.'

'Alright. If you say so.'

'So what is it? You a nonce?'

'No.'

'Child killer? Woman beater? Copper?'

Frank glanced across the yard to Mike, who was now standing with his back to them, looking the other way. 'No,' he said. 'I told you. I'm sorry if I don't look like a financial guy to you, but there's not a whole lot I can do about that, is there?'

The man looked at him for a moment, then slowly

nodded. 'Alright. Alright. We just got to be careful round here, you know? You never know who's who. We've had all sorts in here. Paedos, child rapists, kiddy killers, filth. Not one of them comes in here and admits who they are. But we always find out, yeah? You can't trust no-one in here. Just remember that.'

Frank watched as the men walked back over to the other side of the yard and re-joined their friends. The sun still shone brightly, but Frank'd had enough of being outside.

He never thought a prison cell would provide a sense of welcome relief, but as he walked over the threshold and into his room — a moniker which made it feel more homely and less depressing — he immediately felt safer. While the yard could be an open free-for-all, his solo cell provided him at least a little protection.

He closed the door behind him, confident in the knowledge it could only be opened by him from the inside during allotted times, or by a prison officer from the outside. Letting out a sigh, he threw himself onto his bed, in the hope of getting some sleep.

The second his back hit the bed, he was in instant agony. He roared with pain as he rolled off the bed, feeling the searing sensation with every movement.

He stumbled to his feet and looked back at the bed, which was now soaked with blood. From here, he could now see the razor blades that'd been pushed into his mattress, having pierced the sheet — and his back — the moment he'd laid down.

He turned slightly to look at his reflection in the safety mirror, trying to reach his arm up behind him to pull out one of the blades embedded in his back, but the pain was agonising.

He fumbled at the door, finally managing to open it before staggering out onto the landing.

'Help!' he groaned, the searing pain in his back making it difficult to even breathe.

He looked down the landing, noticing Mike at the other end, looking at him. He made no attempt to respond, didn't come to his aid. Instead, Mike smiled and walked off.

9

Wendy never ceased to be amazed at the work which could be done on a dead body to make it appear at least a little less dreadful than it had before. In the case of the body they presumed to be Matthew Hulford, it had been prepared for identification by his parents by heavily cushioning the back of his head and leaving only his face and the front of his hair visible. The drape had been brought right up to his chin, hiding the slash wound across his neck. The back of his head, and other areas of his body which had received heavy blows had been covered, so as to protect his dignity and the memories of his parents.

In some more extreme cases, visual identification by the family wouldn't be possible under any circumstances, and DNA matches had to be relied on. But Matthew's parents had specifically asked to see the body, and the mortuary team had been confident they could prepare the body in an adequate way.

Dale and Cleo Hulford were briefed on what to expect

before they went into the room, and had been given a good level of preparation, particularly as Jack and Wendy both felt there was no doubt the body was Matthew. In their minds, the focus had moved on from identification of the body to identifying why someone would want to murder a seemingly happy, shy but friendly lad who appeared to have no enemies or reason for someone to want him dead.

Wendy watched as Dale Hulford clutched on to his wife, and in that moment she sensed the man knew what was coming. In any case, most people who came through here hadn't seen a dead body before, and that was often enough of a shock in itself. To at least half expect that the body might be that of your own child would be enough to send anyone into an extreme fit of stress and anxiety.

As Dale and Cleo were led into the room, Wendy watched on, both needing to record the identification for professional purposes, but at the same time not in the slightest relishing the prospect of watching a happy family fall apart in front of her eyes. It was a job which meant she saw the best and worst of society, and all of the ups and downs of human emotion. Without a shadow of a doubt, though, this was by far the worst aspect of the job.

In the case of the body lying on the table in the room in front of them, Wendy didn't need the official written or verbal confirmation as to whether Cleo and Dale Hulford recognised his identity. Dale's hand shooting to his mouth as Cleo clung on desperately to him in fits of sobbing told her everything she needed to know.

10

It had taken some time for Cleo Hulford to be calmed to a state where Jack and Wendy could speak to her about the next steps. Wendy couldn't even begin to imagine what it must feel like for them to be in this situation, and she thought back to her own miscarriage — the closest she'd come to what Cleo and Dale were going through, and the closest she ever hoped to come.

Once things had settled a little, Jack, Wendy and the assigned Family Liaison Officer sat together in one of Mildenheath Police's 'casual' rooms — essentially an interview suite, but far less intimidating and much more suited to speaking with witnesses, family members and those who weren't being formally cautioned.

By now, Cleo Hulford had moved on to the quiet stage of grieving, staring blankly at the wall in front of her, her eyes red and her face pale as she occasionally re-computed what had happened and descended into another flood of tears. Dale, on the other hand, had tried to remain stoic and support his wife, but Jack and Wendy knew from experience that this had to end at some point, in much the same way as shaking up a bottle of fizzy drink with the cap still on would eventually result in an explosion.

Each bereaved family was assigned a Family Liaison Officer who'd be their point of contact throughout an investigation, and who was trained in empathy and had particular people skills which meant they could gain the trust of the family and work with them at a particularly difficult time. It was a role Wendy felt she'd never be able to do, and she felt especially relieved that Jack Culverhouse hadn't considered it to be one of his strengths either.

'So, what we need to do is to find out a bit more about Matthew,' Jack said, addressing the Hulfords.

'Before we do,' Cleo said, 'I need to know what happened.'

'In what sense?' Wendy asked, a look passing between her and Jack. They both knew exactly what Cleo Hulford was asking, and hoped stalling her might give them a precious few seconds to formulate their answer. Every parent had a right to know how their child had died, but there was often no delicate way of describing a murder.

'I mean how did he die?'

Jack took a deep breath before speaking. 'Until the post-mortem's done we won't know for definite, but early indications are that we're probably looking at multiple heavy trauma, but the likely cause of death was a laceration to the neck.'

'Someone beat him to death and slit his throat,' Dale Hulford said, his voice almost a whisper.

'I suppose there are a number of ways of phrasing it,' Jack replied.

'Are we talking some random psycho?' Cleo asked. 'If there's someone out there attacking random people for no reason, you should be out there looking for them, not wasting your time with us.'

Wendy swallowed. 'We're not entirely sure this was a random attack.'

The ensuing silence was deafening. Matthew's parents looked like the air had been kicked out of their lungs.

'What do you mean?' Cleo asked.

Jack took another deep breath. 'There's no easy way to say this, but at the moment we're working on the assumption that Matthew was deliberately targeted.'

'Why?' Cleo whispered, after a few seconds.

'That's what we need to find out. And with any luck, that'll lead us to who. Now, you mentioned that Matthew had been over at his friend's house. Connor French, wasn't it?'

Dale Hulford's eyes narrowed. 'Yeah, but Connor's a good lad. They were inseparable. He wouldn't—'

Culverhouse raised his hand slightly. 'Oh no, I'm not suggesting anything of the sort. We're just trying to find out more about Matthew, who his friends were, where he liked to go, all those things. Trying to build a picture of who he was.'

Dale shrugged. 'He only really had Connor, as far as

friends go. He was over there with him all the time. Computer games. They've both loved them for years.'

'Did Connor ever come over to yours?'

'Sometimes, but nowhere near as often as Matt went there,' Dale replied. 'Connor had the latest console, see. We were a bit more realistic on that front. We wanted him to wait for a bit, at least until the prices came down. Maybe if we…'

'You can't think like that,' Wendy said. 'Trust me, a games console won't have made a difference. What was Matthew like as a person?'

They watched as a chain of emotions crossed his parents' faces: pride, admiration, love, followed by the realisation they'd never see him again, never speak to him again.

'He was a lovely boy,' Dale said, his voice touched by emotion. 'Always hugged and kissed his mum. What boy of his age still does that? He was a clever lad. Did well at school. Didn't even need to try. Just came naturally to him. He was never in any trouble.'

'Did he have a girlfriend at all?' Wendy asked.

Dale and Cleo looked at each other. 'Jenny,' Cleo said, after a few seconds of deafening silence.

'Jenny? Is that Matthew's girlfriend?'

Cleo nodded. 'They'd been seeing each other on and off for a little while. She's… she seemed to be a lot keener on Matthew than he was on her.'

'How do you mean?'

Cleo took a deep breath, then let out a huge sigh. 'I don't know what it was. Maybe she's just one of these people who gets really attached and plans her wedding with the first boy she meets, but she seemed really... clingy. She used to come over here looking for Matthew, and we'd have to say he'd gone out. He was at Connor's, but we'd just say we didn't know where he was. If he didn't want to spend every waking minute with her, that was his decision.'

Dale interjected. 'She made a comment to Cleo about being terrible parents because we didn't know where he was and what he was up to. Cleo closed the door on her. That was the last time we saw her.'

'And when was this?' Wendy asked.

'Nearly two weeks ago,' Cleo replied. 'Not the last we heard of her, though. Matthew let slip that she'd made some daft remark about them having children. I think it shook him up a bit.'

'And how were things left between them?'

'Fine. If you want to put it that way. Dale and I thought he might finally give her the heave-ho, but there we are.'

'Do you happen to know what Jenny's surname is?' Wendy asked.

'Yes. It's Blake.'

Wendy made a note of the name. Both she and Jack knew where they'd be heading next.

11

Much like the Hulfords, the Blake family lived in a respectable area of town, in a cul-de-sac the police were barely aware existed. Although they weren't far from town, as they stepped out of the car and onto the Blakes' driveway, there was silence except for the birds in the trees.

By the time Jack and Wendy got to Jenny Blake's house, it was apparent that she already knew what'd happened to Matthew. Her face, and those of her parents, were clearly pained at what had happened, and Jenny looked more like someone who'd lost her husband of twenty years than a girl barely into adulthood whose boyfriend of only a few months had died.

Jenny's father led them into the living room, before offering them tea or coffee — naturally declined. 'Oh, I'm sorry,' he said. 'Where are my manners. I'm Clive, this is my wife Aretha. Sorry — don't quite know where my brain is this morning.'

'Don't worry,' Wendy replied with a sympathetic smile. 'It's understandable. We're really sorry for your loss. All of you.'

'Thank you,' Jenny's mum, Aretha, replied. 'It's just... a bit of a shock, that's all.'

Clive put his hand on his wife's shoulder and gave it a reassuring squeeze. Jenny was sitting on the sofa, her face almost blank, as if the shock had set in and she was struggling to process what had happened. Wendy sat down next to her.

'Jenny, do you feel comfortable having a chat with us? We just need to find out a bit more about Matthew and the sort of person he was.'

'Uh. Yeah. Okay.'

'Would you like to speak in private?'

'I dunno. I...'

'It's okay, sweetie,' Clive said, coming to her. 'We can be here if you want us to be. If that'd make you more comfortable.'

'We'll try not to make it too arduous,' Wendy said. 'I know it's difficult, but the more we know about Matthew, the more likely we'll be to find out who did this to him.'

'Christ. Sends a shiver down your spine, doesn't it?' Clive said. 'All this talk, I mean. About him being... you know.'

'Murdered, Dad. You can say it.'

'I know. I know. I'm just not sure I want to.'

Wendy cocked her head slightly and looked at Jenny. 'What can you tell us about Matthew? What sort of person was he?'

Jenny seemed to think about this for a few moments before speaking. 'I wanted to save him,' she said, finally.

'Save him? From what?'

'From himself. From what he was turning into.'

Wendy flicked a look at Jack, then asked, 'Sorry. What do you mean?'

Jenny sighed. 'You'll find out anyway. You always do. Matt dealt drugs. Him and his mate Connor.'

There was an audible gasp from Aretha, and Clive put his hand on his wife's shoulder again to reassure her.

'What sort of drugs?' Wendy asked.

Jenny shrugged. 'Whatever people wanted. Mostly just weed and poppers. Tabs. He didn't tend to get too involved in the harder stuff. Mostly because Connor said it'd be too dangerous. Too many bad people involved. All he was doing was trying to earn some money so we could get a place and settle down together.'

'Okay. Now listen, we're not here to pass judgement and we're not investigating any drug dealing. We've got bigger things to focus on here, so you can be honest with us. Were you involved at all?'

Jenny shook her head. 'No. Never. I didn't want him involved in all that either. I mean, it wasn't anything major. He didn't get into the hard stuff, and didn't really do anything himself apart from a bit of weed every now and then.'

'So it was him and Connor? What was the supply chain? Did they grow it?'

'No. They had a guy. I never knew his name. Someone who wanted to lie low. Matt and Connor were his in-between guys. They'd buy off him and sell it on. He sold it to them for a bit less than normal because they kept him anonymous, and sold it on for a bit more than normal so they didn't get all the cheap skagheads who'd cause trouble.'

Clive uttered a whispered 'Jesus Christ'.

'And you don't know who this man is?' Wendy asked her.

'No, I swear down. He wouldn't even tell me. That was the whole point. It was all kept under wraps.'

'Okay. And did Matthew and Connor ever do anything to upset this man, do you think?'

Jenny shook her head. 'No. No chance. He was the one making them money. Without his stuff, they wouldn't have had anything. There's no way either of them was going to start growing at home, and no-one else would supply to them at that price. But seriously, that's all I know. I wanted to get him out of it. I could see which way it was going to go. No-one ever comes out of this in a good way. I just wanted him to pack it all in and get a normal job. He wanted that, too. He was about to pack it all in.'

'Is that seriously all you know?' Jack asked, his tone of voice indicating that he didn't entirely believe her.

'Yeah it is. I wanted to keep out of it. I don't want anything to do with drugs, do I? I've never even tried puff. It's not my scene. Trust me, the only one who knows anything is Connor. He's the one you want to be talking to.'

12

Jack and Wendy left the Blakes' house feeling as if they knew far more about Matthew Hulford, and at the same time much less. One thing was for certain: they had a lead and a direction. It seemed likely to both of them that drugs would be involved somewhere along the line as the reason behind Matthew's murder, but they were still a long way from having any conclusive focus.

Even a vague indication of a drugs background wouldn't lead them directly to their killer. There was a lot more that would need to be done to even identify a solid motive, let alone a suspect. However, if Connor French was not only Matthew's closest friend but also his fellow drug dealer, it seemed likely that he would at least be able to shed some light on both motives and suspects.

Jack and Wendy hadn't been particularly surprised at the revelation that a seemingly model child had been caught up in something far more sinister. It was a story they'd seen numerous times over the years, and which they knew they'd see again. Too many parents saw their children through younger eyes, viewing them as incapable of harbouring dark secrets or keeping things from them. The truth, however, was quite different. Too few adults looked back with complete honesty at how they were at that age, and almost all were stunned to discover that their children were capable of far more than they realised.

Their first impression of Connor French on arriving at his house wasn't that of a hardened drug dealer. It was — at best — a fragile kid who briefly took the wrong path. Connor was in floods of desperate tears as Jack and Wendy walked through into the kitchen, where the young lad was perched on a stool at the breakfast bar, head in his arms.

'We've been trying to get him to eat and drink,' Connor's father said, having closed the door and followed them in. 'We couldn't get him to leave his bedroom for the first hour.'

They watched as Connor's mum comforted him, her own face a picture of desperation and brokenness as she realised — perhaps for the first time — that there was nothing she could do to fix this or make her son feel better.

'Connor, it's the police,' his dad said. 'They want to ask a few questions about Matt.'

Connor's sobs gradually slowed to the point where he was able to give himself a couple of seconds to speak between breaths. He looked at them through scarlet eyes, his cheeks red raw, hair dampening at the roots. 'You need to find the fucker who did this,' he said.

'Connor. Language,' his mum replied, trying to make the rebuke sound as gentle and reassuring as possible.

'That's certainly our intention,' Jack said. 'But in order to do that we need to find out as much information as possible. Even little things can make a big difference, whether they seem like it at the time or not.'

'Do you feel up to talking to us?' Wendy asked. 'The sooner we're able to get some more information, the quicker we can find the person who did this.'

Connor looked up at her and nodded.

'Alright,' Wendy said. 'Do you want to go somewhere private, perhaps? We can go wherever you feel more comfortable.' For her, it was key that Connor was able to speak openly and honestly, and she realised he might not be keen on revealing he was a bit-part drug dealer in front of his parents.

Connor swallowed. 'Yeah. Maybe,' he said.

His parents seemed to pick up on the subtext and made gestures to leave.

'We'll just be through here if you need us Connor, okay?' his mum said, before they both left the room and headed through the hallway and into the lounge.

'How are you feeling?' Wendy asked him.

Connor shrugged. 'How'm I meant to feel?'

'I'll be honest, I don't know. I can imagine it came as quite a shock.'

'Yeah. You can say that again.'

'Matthew was with you last night, wasn't he?'

'Yeah. For a bit.'

'What were you doing?'

'Playing games at mine. We used to do it quite a lot.'

Jack and Wendy could see the moment painted on Connor's face when he realised he wouldn't see his friend again.

'It's okay,' Wendy said. 'I know this must be hard for you. But we need to get a solid picture of what happened. What time did Matthew get to yours?'

'Uh, about six, I think?'

'And when did he leave?'

'He usually goes home about ten-ish. I didn't look at the clock.'

'And how does he get home?'

'He walks it. It's less than five minutes.'

'What game were you playing?' Jack asked.

Connor shrugged. 'All sorts. FIFA. Watch Dogs. Far Cry. Depends how we feel.'

'And you played all three last night?'

Connor shrugged again. 'Dunno. Don't really remember.'

Jack looked away and gently nodded. 'Alright. Well maybe we can jog your memory. Maybe you weren't playing any of those games. Maybe it wasn't any game at all. Maybe — just maybe — you were out wandering the streets, pushing drugs.' He looked back at Connor and saw a flicker of something cross his face.

'Well no,' Connor replied.

'Oh right. Had a night off last night, did you? Listen, Connor. We ain't stupid. It's literally our job to find things out. And if what you tell us doesn't tally with what we've already found out, things tend not to go too well.'

The silence in the kitchen seemed to last forever, Connor holding his breath and his tongue for as long as he could. 'Alright,' he said eventually, the weight visibly lifting from his young shoulders. 'It's just a bit of puff. Nothing heavy. Never enough to get done for intent to supply.'

'Intent's got nothing to do with quantity, Connor. Look the word up in the dictionary. But listen, we ain't here to nick you for drugs. We've got bigger fish to fry. We need to find out who killed Matt and why. Forgive me for sounding like a silly old duffer here, but I genuinely can't remember the last time I investigated the death of a drug dealer that wasn't drug-related somehow. Who's your supplier?'

Connor let out an almost offended laugh, and looked at Jack and Wendy as if they'd just asked him how big his penis was. 'No offence, but I ain't telling you that.'

Jack smiled. 'Trust me, I'm a long way past being offended. About thirty years past it. Nothing you say needs to go further than this room, you know.'

'Oh yeah, right. 'Cos you're not gonna run out of here and go speak to him next, are you.'

'Bloke, is it?'

Connor swallowed. 'He's got nothing to do with it. You'll just have to take my word for that.'

'What, like I had to take your word you were sitting in your bedroom playing Tetris?'

'He's got no reason to want Matt hurt. Total opposite,

if anything. We keep the supply line silent, he doesn't get the hassle. We're doing him a favour. Last thing he wants is you lot sniffing round, so there's no way in hell he'd do something like this.'

'What if it's a test? For you, I mean,' Wendy said, reading a message that'd just come through on her phone.

'It ain't like that. We've proven ourselves enough. Trust me. Me and Matt never wanted to get into anything heavy. He respects that. At the same time, he knows he ain't gonna get the big guns round looking for him over a bit of puff. Matt was my best mate. We'd been best mates ever since we were kids. Trust me, if I had any idea who'd done this to him, I'd tell you. You think I'm going to keep it to myself if I knew who could've killed my best mate?'

Jack raised an eyebrow. 'The way things have gone so far, nothing would surprise me.'

'Connor, did Matt have a mobile phone?' Wendy asked, deliberately changing the subject.

'Well yeah, obviously.'

'Did he bring it with him last night?'

'Yeah. He left it here, actually.'

'He left it?'

'Yeah. Not on purpose, obviously. I found it a little while after he went home.'

'Did you keep it switched on?' Wendy asked, already knowing the answer.

'Nah, it'd run out of battery by the time I found it. I thought I'd walk over first thing and give it back.'

'Why didn't you charge it for him?'

''Cos it's an iPhone and I've only got a Samsung charger.'

'Can we see it?' Wendy asked.

Connor shrugged. 'Yeah. Alright. I'll go get it.'

She watched as Connor walked down the hallway and jogged up the stairs. 'That was Ryan,' she whispered to Jack. 'She texted me to say Matt's phone geolocation shows he was here last night. It goes off the grid about half-past ten and hasn't been seen since. Tallies with it running out of charge.'

Jack nodded. 'Alright. But still, what kid of his age forgets his phone, only lives a couple of minutes' walk away and still doesn't come straight back for it?'

Wendy shrugged. 'Maybe he didn't realise until he got home. You saw what his parents were like. I imagine they're the sort of people to tell him he can manage a few hours without his phone.'

'Either that or he met his killer on the way.'

Wendy raised her eyebrows and nodded. A moment later, they heard Connor coming back down the stairs. He put the phone down on the side.

'We're going to need to bag this and take it with us,' Wendy said, half expecting Connor to protest. Instead, he just shrugged.

'Alright,' he said. 'You won't be able to get anything off it, though.'

13

As the sun started to set on a long day, Jack felt his eyes stinging with tiredness.

'Right,' he said, addressing his team. 'I've had enough for one day. We've made good progress, but we've still got a long way to go. Steve, can you organise for surveillance to be put on Connor French, please. The boy's running scared. Whether he thinks he's next or not, I don't know, but I'm pretty certain he's going to make contact with someone at some point. We haven't got the budget for a physical tail, but let's get his phone and social media monitored. See who he's talking to. Live intercepts if we can.'

Steve nodded and wrote down a few notes. In an age where concerns over privacy and personal data were rising at the same rate as a desire for tougher law enforcement, it was impossible to balance the two. Quite often, the same people who complained about the police not being able to catch enough criminals were the same ones who waxed lyrical about personal privacy and being able to lock down their entire lives from prying eyes. Unfortunately, the two didn't quite go together.

'We've got Matt Hulford's mobile phone bagged and sent off to Milton House for analysis, with my apologies to Detective Sergeant Knight for giving her boyfriend overtime. On the plus side, the corner shop are doing an offer on double-A batteries. For now, if there's any contact whatsoever with Matt's parents, we're keeping the drugs thing on the down low. I'll go over and speak to them in the morning about that. It's not something I fancy much after the day I've had, and I'm pretty sure they'd feel the same.'

'What if someone tells them in the meantime?' DS Ryan Mackenzie asked.

'They won't. Connor and Jenny are under strict instruction. And anyway, if they find out before, they find out before. Let's face it, anyone could've told them at any point up until now, and until we've got more certainty that drugs have got anything to do with his death, it's best we sleep on it first. That's not the sort of shitshow we want to be directing at the moment. I'll go over and see them in the morning.'

'Anything else?' Steve asked.

Jack shook his head. 'I don't think so. Don't reckon there's a whole lot more we can do right now. Might be worth giving the social media team a nudge, though. Probably not going to be all that helpful to have people blabbing all over the local groups about drugs links.

That's the last thing the family are going to need right now. Won't be helpful for us, either.'

It was true to say that local social media groups were often a cesspit of commentary. It was a sad indictment on society that the invention of Facebook and Twitter had made ordinary people confuse the distinction between having a right to an opinion and other people having the right to ignore it. With the advent of social media, everyone seemed to not only think they were an expert, but they also appeared to labour under the misapprehension that anybody else on earth cared as much about their opinion as they did, even if it did give them some momentary respite from their joyless existence.

'Right,' Jack said. 'On that note, I'm fucking off home.'

14

Jack felt the stiffness in his shoulders and lower back as he unlocked the front door — the same stiffness he got after any long, stress-filled day. For many years, home had provided no real respite from those sorts of days, and he'd instead chosen to spend even longer hours at the office, preferring the dull, monotonous routine of work over the loneliness of an empty house. Now, though, the house was far from empty, and it was only going to get fuller.

'Put the guns down, it's only me,' he called as he closed the door behind him. He walked through into the living room and found Emily lying on one of the sofas. 'You alright, love? You look like shit.'

'Wow. Thanks. I feel it.'

'Still struggling?' he asked, planting a kiss on her forehead.

'It's alright. Good days and bad days.'

'I'm guessing today's a bad one.'

'Oh yes.'

'Do you want chicken soup?'

'Why would I want chicken soup?' Emily asked, her face curling.

Jack shrugged. 'I dunno. Your mum used to get bad days when she was pregnant with you. For some reason, one day she worked out she had a real craving for chicken soup. Two bloody hours I spent, running round every supermarket in Mildenheath, trying to get all the ingredients. I got home, and you know what she said to me? She said "Why didn't you just buy a tin from the first supermarket?" And that's when I knew I'd had an even longer day than she had. Tell you what, though. I got every single one of those ingredients and I stood there in that kitchen and I made her chicken soup. It worked like a dream. Every time she had morning sickness or a shit day, chicken soup helped.'

'Have we got any?' Emily asked.

'Well, no. At least I don't think so. I can go and get some, though.'

Emily chuckled. 'No, don't. As much as I love the idea of you jogging round all the supermarkets looking for herbs you've never heard of, I really haven't got a craving for chicken soup.'

'Thank god for that. I thought for a minute we'd have history repeating itself.'

'Not likely.'

'Oh I dunno. You're pretty similar in a lot of ways.'

'I don't think so,' Emily said, diverting her attention towards the television.

'No, you are. She used to do that, too. Lying on the

sofa, watching TV when things felt bad. Used to take her mind off it, she said.'

Emily sat up, picked up the remote control and switched the TV off. 'Yeah. Well, I've been doing enough of that today. And it's killing my back anyway.'

Jack smiled. 'Your mum used to say the same thing. Obviously runs in the genes.'

'For fuck's sake, Dad!' Emily barked, stunning Jack into silence. 'Can you please stop telling me how much like her I am? Don't you get it? I don't *want* to be like her. There's a reason I came back here and didn't go off with her. I know what she's like. What she's *really* like. I don't want anything to do with her, and I don't want anything to do with her fucking genes!'

Jack watched as Emily pulled herself to her feet and wandered off into the kitchen, listening as he heard her pulling pots and pans out of the cupboards and lighting the hob. He wanted to walk in and help her, tell her to sit down and rest. But he knew that wouldn't do any good. That'd only make her more determined to show him that she was actually fine and was more than capable of doing things for herself, without the help of anyone else.

In that moment, Jack realised she was right: those weren't Helen's genes at all. They were his. Helen had a tendency to run away from trouble and pretend it wasn't happening. More often than not, she'd run away to somewhere even more dangerous, feeling a false sense of safety whilst simply doubling up on her problems. Jack, on the other hand, tried to face adversity head on. If someone told him he couldn't do something, that made him only more determined to damn well make sure he did it.

He'd never quite known how to deal with Helen, and that had caused a huge number of problems over the years. Even now, he felt he'd never really known her. When Emily had come back into his life and shown signs of her personality traits, he'd panicked and worried whether he'd ever be able to build a relationship with his daughter. But that had all changed.

He watched through the kitchen door as Emily started chopping onions and garlic, knowing full well that she didn't know any more than him what she was going to end up cooking. But she was going to damn well cook, if only to prove a point. He looked at her and realised there was far less of Helen in her than he'd thought, and far more of himself. And in that moment, he felt a growing but satisfying realisation that things were going to be alright after all.

15

The next morning should've provided a sense of clarity and a new purpose, but in reality all it had done was make Jack feel anxious.

If he was honest with himself, he knew the real reason for wanting to delay visiting Matt Hulford's parents again yesterday evening was purely because he knew it would tear them apart. Their world had already collapsed on being told their son was dead — murdered — and the realisation that their model child had been a drug dealer, most likely killed because of his lifestyle, would deal them another severe hammer blow.

Jack had already seen enough lives and families torn apart to last him a lifetime. And that wasn't even including his own. He didn't know if he was just going soft in his old age, but the cold, removed 'simply business' Jack Culverhouse appeared to have faded into the background recently. Not that he'd admit it to anyone.

For Wendy, the morning's task was a little more

prosaic. Although no-one liked having to be the one to give families bad news about their loved ones, Wendy was under no illusions. As far as she was concerned, this was all part of the job. An unfortunate part, yes, but that was by the by.

They'd decided to head out to the Hulford house in Wendy's car, which allowed Jack to observe her a little more closely. He recalled the day Wendy Knight first joined his team: an apprehensive young detective, keen to put the world to rights and shake up the system. They all started like that. Even he had. They all thought time spent in the system would allow them to see and analyse its weaknesses, giving them the insight to make the changes that needed to be made. But the truth was, the system corrupts. Before you knew where you were, you'd become a product of it yourself.

Maybe it was a result of him softening in his old age just as Wendy had become fully entrenched in her chosen career. Perhaps it was something to do with his family circumstances having changed whilst Wendy's seemed to have stagnated. But regardless of the reasoning he gave, he couldn't deny the realisation that he'd softened and she'd hardened.

'I don't imagine this'll be much fun,' he said, as they pulled out of the car park and headed in the direction of the Hulford house.

'Nope. Probably the first time a family like that has realised the world of drugs is right on their doorstep.'

Jack laughed. 'I doubt that. Just look at all the London commuters getting off the train every night. Accountants, analysts, city boys, all wide-eyed with white powder under their noses. Course, all's well and good until it's a young lad doing a bit of puff behind a kebab shop. And don't even get me started on the housewives keeping themselves perked up with painkillers and tranquillisers.'

'I guess a lot of people would argue painkillers and tranquillisers are legal.'

'Yep. And without questioning why. They'll happily take a shot of morphine without even knowing it's heroin under a different name. You and I know as much as anyone that something being legal doesn't make it right. Slavery was legal.'

'Bloody hell. You been up all night watching YouTube or something?' Wendy said, chuckling to herself.

'No. Just saying, that's all. Why?'

'Why? Because you seem to have woken up as Martin Luther King. That's why.'

'Yeah, well I don't intend to get shot if that's what you're getting at.'

There was an uncomfortable silence as they recognised the elephant in the room: that Jack had been shot at whilst apprehending the Mildenheath Ripper years earlier, only for his young protégé Luke Baxter to put himself between Jack and the bullet, losing his life in the process.

'I imagine the parents will've had some sort of inkling,' Wendy said. 'Even if it looks like they're completely oblivious, I don't see how any parents could be. They must have at least suspected something, if only on a subconscious level.'

'You'd be surprised,' Jack muttered to the window,

watching the rain run down in rivulets. 'I don't think parents pay as much attention to their kids as they used to. Everyone's so bloody busy all the time. Plus the kids can hide what they're doing now they've all got smartphones and everything's online. Not like the old days when you had to sneak down to the phone box or hope people only called when your parents were out.'

'I dunno. You can put a lot of blocks and parental controls on devices nowadays. It's easy enough for parents to keep tabs on what kids are doing.'

'Yeah, but most don't. And anyway, where do you draw the line? Matthew Hulford was hardly a nine-year-old kid with his first iPod, was he? He'd left school. Old enough to pay taxes. Old enough to join the army. Old enough to get himself into a whole shitheap of trouble and end up assassinated in the woods.'

Jack's thoughts turned momentarily to his daughter, Emily. She'd seemed to him, just months earlier, to still be a child. But the revelation she was pregnant with a child of her own had dragged Jack's mental image of her kicking and screaming into adulthood, even if she was barely fifteen herself. Although she was still a child on paper, there could be no doubt that this was the sort of situation that would make anyone grow up pretty damn quickly.

They arrived at the Hulford house and walked up the driveway to the front door for the second time — both occasions to deal a hammer blow to Matthew's parents. Dale Hulford recognised them immediately and welcomed them in, guiding them through to the living room.

'Have you got some news?' he asked once they'd all sat down. 'Have you found out who did it?'

Jack and Wendy shared a momentary look. 'Not yet,' Wendy said. 'Although we do think we have a potential lead.'

Dale and Cleo Hulford steadied themselves and looked at Wendy. 'Okay,' Dale said. 'Go on.'

Wendy swallowed and looked down at the carpet for a moment before speaking. 'We're looking into the possibility that Matthew's death may have been drugs-related.'

Matthew's parents looked at her blankly.

'No, that's not possible,' Dale said. 'Not drugs. Matt didn't take drugs.'

'Drugs?' Cleo asked. 'But you told us he'd been murdered. His hands were tied behind his back. He'd been beaten.'

'Yes. That's correct,' Wendy replied. 'We don't know for certain whether or not Matthew took drugs himself, but we have good reason to believe he was involved in the supply of drugs, and we're looking into the possibility that this could have given someone a motive to murder him.'

'No,' Cleo said firmly. 'No. That's not true. Matthew didn't deal drugs. That's ridiculous. He was a good boy. That's not him at all. You're wrong.'

'Cleo,' her husband whispered.

'No, Dale. They're wrong. They've got their facts wrong.'

'I'm sorry, Mrs Hulford,' Wendy said. 'But we've got witness statements that have told us that. And they're not the sort of people who'd want to lie about it. They've potentially incriminated themselves by telling us. There's no doubt in our minds whatsoever that Matthew was involved in selling drugs.'

Jack and Wendy watched as Cleo Hulford crumbled in front of them.

Half an hour later, Wendy parked her car at Mildenheath Police Station and Jack glanced at his watch, as if he hadn't been acutely aware of the time all morning and hadn't had his mind firmly on the appointment he'd made.

'Ah, ten o'clock,' he said. 'I've got to be somewhere at half past. Can you brief the team on what the Hulfords said? I should be back about lunchtime.'

'Oh. Yeah, sure,' Wendy said. 'Everything okay? Emily got a scan?'

'No. No, nothing like that. Don't worry. I'll be back in a couple of hours.'

Jack got out of her car and walked over to his own, feeling the adrenaline coursing through his legs at the thought of what was to come.

16

Jack switched off his car engine and looked up at the building in front of him. He wasn't the sort of person to feel overawed or nervous in places like this. He'd dealt with some pretty nasty people in his time, and it was a sad indictment that — in many ways — it was just another day at work. But this time it was different. This time he did feel nervous.

He wasn't sure what he wanted to say to Frank. He'd had countless four-a.m. conversations with him in his head over the past weeks, but none of them had given him the answers he was looking for.

If he was being honest with himself, he wasn't sure he wanted to know the truth. It was bad enough knowing that one of his longest-serving and most trusted colleagues had betrayed him in the worst possible way, without needing to know the details.

The fact was that any form of police corruption completely undermined the rule of law and order. Once the checks and balances broke down or were found to be corruptible, everything fell apart. It was one thing to have a justice system which failed to catch its criminals; it was another entirely when elements of that system actively worked for the other side.

It could have been almost understandable if it'd been a young, impressionable officer who'd had their head turned by money or the lure of a quick payday. Perhaps someone who'd joined the police force then decided it wasn't for them. But that wasn't the case with Frank. He'd been a loyal and dedicated police officer for most of his life, and had been on the verge of retirement after a long and distinguished career. Why had he chosen to throw that all away and go down in history as a bent copper?

Try as he might, Jack couldn't shake the suspicion that Frank might have been working against his colleagues for much longer. It was no secret that Jack had been trying to nail McCann for a number of years. The whole team had. Or so he'd thought. But, try as they might, somehow McCann managed to wriggle off the hook every time. It wasn't a thought Jack wanted to entertain, but the possibility that they'd had a mole on side the whole time certainly made a lot of other things fall into place.

Jack had called ahead to let the prison know he'd be visiting. On paper, it was an official police visit. In reality, though, the investigation into Frank's activities was being handled externally. In cases where corruption was involved or suspected, everything had to be investigated by another force, in order to ensure independence and impartiality. Jack wasn't interested in gathering evidence.

Not in an official capacity. As far as he was concerned, this was a private visit, albeit one on his terms.

He waited as the man on the front desk checked and verified his ID, then surrendered his mobile phone and keys, before stepping into a body scanner. A few seconds later, a green light appeared and a prison officer gestured for Jack to follow her.

When they eventually reached the small room, Jack stepped inside to find Frank already seated behind the table.

'There'll be someone just outside,' the officer said.

Jack mumbled his thanks, unable to take his eyes off his old colleague.

'You can sit down,' Frank said, a few seconds after the door had clanged shut.

'I know that. I'm just not sure if I want to.'

'Well you'll have to make your mind up sharpish. I've got so much to be getting on with.'

Jack ignored Frank's attempt at humour. 'You know, I had so many things I wanted to say. Questions I wanted to ask. I had visions of them having to drag me out by my arms because there wouldn't be enough hours in the day to get to the bottom of things. But then I walk in here and see you sitting there in that chair, and you know what I thought? "There's a man who's lost it all." More than anything else, I feel sorry for you. And I think to myself, what's the point? What does it matter? It ain't gonna change anything. What's done is done, you've turned into a sad, miserable little fuck and you'll always be a sad, miserable little fuck.'

Frank shuffled awkwardly in his seat and winced in pain.

'Arse still hurting?' Jack asked.

'Yeah.'

'Good. I hope it gets infected.'

'You came here for a reason, Jack.'

'I thought so too. But now I've seen you, I'm not so sure it matters anymore.'

'I think you and I both know that's not true. Look, I know you're angry. I get that.'

'Angry?'

'What word do you want me to use? There isn't one.'

'I can think of a couple.'

Frank sat silently for a few moments. 'How is everyone?' he asked eventually. 'The team, I mean.'

'What does it matter? You've made it perfectly clear how much they mean to you. If you gave the slightest shit about them, we wouldn't be here having this conversation.'

'Look, Jack, if you've just come here to have a pop and let off some steam, trust me, I totally get that. I don't blame you one bit. But let's not pretend it's anything else, eh?'

'How long?' Jack asked, throwing Frank off balance.

'How long what?'

'How long have you been working for McCann?'

Frank sighed. 'I haven't been working for him. That's not… It wasn't like that.'

'How long?'

'Why does it matter?'

'Because I need to know.'

'Why?'

'The facts need to come out, Frank.'

'They will,' Frank replied, his voice slipping.

Jack looked at him. It was one of those moments where, having known the man for years, he could read a huge amount from the slight variation in his voice. 'Tell me you're fucking joking, Frank,' he said.

'What?'

'You're not going to testify, are you?'

Frank looked away, towards the floor. 'It's not as easy as that,' he said.

'Yes it is. You know that more than anyone. You and I've spent our whole lives trying to put bastards like McCann behind bars. We do this job for a reason, Frank. It's because, deep down, we know what's right and what's wrong. Yes, you might've got sucked in and drawn into something you shouldn't've, and yes, you might have fucked your whole career and your life's work by letting that happen, but *my* career's based on knowing when someone's a good egg or a wrong'un, and I know damn well — as well as you do — that you're not that kind of person.'

'What does it matter? It's done.'

'No it's not. It's nowhere near done, Frank. Sit back and have a look at this. Gary McCann and his criminal empire are still running around out there, doing whatever they like. Do you want to know where he is? He's sitting at home with his feet up. He's a free man, yet again. And somehow, somehow, you're the one banged up in prison for what he did. A copper with years of service putting cunts like him away. Do you really think he gives a shit? Do you think he's giving you a moment's thought while he's sitting at home, sipping his Ovaltine, watching Homes Under the Hammer? Frank, I hate to break it to you mate, but you've got no choice. If you're entire life's not going to be thrown away and wasted, you need to do the right thing. You owe it to me. You owe it to the team. To the entire police force. To society. But most of all, you owe it to yourself.'

'It's not as easy as that.'

'Yes it is. Don't let that arsehole get into your head. He's only got power while no-one challenges it. And right now, you're the only one who can end that.'

Frank sighed again. 'Is that all you're here for? You want me to testify against McCann so you can finally feel like your career's been worth it?'

'This ain't about me, Frank.'

'Come off it, yes it is. You've wanted to send McCann down since day one. Every single time he's come across our radar, you've got more and more desperate. This is what it's all about, isn't it? You're not bothered about redemption or justice. Not in the conventional sense. You just want to get one over on Gary McCann and win gloating rights.'

'You're bloody lucky someone's already torn you a new arsehole, Frank. It means I don't have to. This isn't about me. It's about what McCann has done to me, to you, to Mildenheath. Do you want to go down as the bent copper who enabled a criminal empire, or the man who dedicated his life to fighting crime, got sucked in, but turned himself around and helped bring a major criminal to justice?'

'Jack, I...'

'No, Frank. I don't wanna hear it. I've said my bit.'

17

Jack arrived back at the office just before midday, and decided to call a briefing before anyone disappeared off for lunch.

'Okay,' he said, 'I understand DS Knight has appraised you all of how we managed to shatter Dale and Cleo Hulford's perfect existence for the second day in a row, so full marks to us for that. Steve, how's the surveillance going?'

Steve Wing leaned back in his chair and sighed. 'Not much to tell, boss. Hasn't called anyone, texted anyone. Nothing. He put an "RIP Matt Hulford" post on Facebook and tagged Matthew into it, but as of yet he hasn't replied.'

A rumbled of laughter rippled round the room. Dark humour was always appreciated in the job, wherever it could be found.

'Debbie, any other mobile phones registered to Connor or Matthew?' Jack asked.

DC Weston shook her head. 'Not that we can find. There might be unregistered phones in use, but triangulation isn't showing us signs of any devices other than those already known to us as owned by the family. I'd say they probably used their own mobiles for dealing, but kept it on the down low by using encrypted messaging apps. We could probably find out easily enough by asking Connor, but do we think he'd reveal all?'

'Depends if he wants us to find out who killed his mate, doesn't it?' Jack replied.

'Triangulation's showing Matt and Connor were at Connor's house on the night he died,' Ryan Mackenzie said, shuffling in her chair. 'Interestingly, it looks like they were telling the truth. Neither phone leaves at any point in the evening. Matt's goes off about half ten, like Connor said. But it looks like they did stay in after all.

'Right. DS Knight. We've got news back from loverboy, have we?'

'We've got news back from tech forensics,' Wendy said, not rising to the bait. 'Matt's phone's secured with an alphanumeric passcode. That means both letters and numbers, making it almost impossible to crack. The number of possibilities is huge, and we only need to get it wrong three times before it locks us out permanently. No fingerprint recognition, no facial recognition, so we can't even make use of that.'

'Fucking brilliant,' Jack replied, plonking himself down on the edge of a desk. 'Can we call the manufacturer? Apple, is it? Ask them to break into it. Or the phone network.'

'Doesn't work like that, unfortunately. Apple are notoriously unwilling to compromise the privacy of their users. They won't unlock phones. Not even for the police.'

'I got onto Sony, too,' Ryan said, 'to find out whether or not Connor's user account was logged in. It was — from six-thirty until a couple of minutes before ten. Active the whole time.'

'Right. So they happened to be playing computer games that evening. Still doesn't give us a whole lot, but it does narrow things down. So we're looking at the most likely option being that Matthew was either ambushed on his walk home, or that he got home — or at least partway home — realised he'd forgotten his mobile, walked back and was ambushed on the way. But neither walk would've taken him anywhere near Mildenheath Woods, would it?'

'No,' Debbie replied. 'Wouldn't make any sense to go that way. I imagine he's either been picked up in a car and taken there, or was planning to meet someone. Perhaps that person killed him.'

'Why would he plan to meet them without taking his phone?' Jack asked.

'Maybe he didn't want to be tracked. If this is all connected with drugs, and if Matt's smart enough to lock down his phone, use encrypted messaging and so on, it's not unreasonable to think he'd be well aware we can track cell site data. Maybe he was keeping his powder dry.'

'Alright. Get onto Connor and the girlfriend again. Find out if he'd arranged to meet anyone. No, scrap that. Tell them we *know* he'd gone to meet someone. Put the pressure on. We might have some luck with the girlfriend, but Connor's only ever fessed up when we've hit him with what we already know. So we go in to him telling him we know Matt'd arranged to meet someone. See what he says.'

The ethics of this approach were questionable to say the least, but none of the team felt the need to question it.

Jack's flow was broken by the ringing of his mobile phone. He glanced down at it, seeing Chief Constable Charles Hawes's name on the screen. 'Right. That'll do for now,' he said. 'Let me take this and I'll be back.'

Jack left the incident room as he took the call, heading in the direction of the Chief Constable's office as he answered.

'Sir.'

'Jack, have you got a sec to come and see me please?'

'Already on my way. Be there in two.'

When Jack reached Hawes's office, he knocked and entered.

He'd always enjoyed a good relationship with Hawes, knowing a large part of the reason he was still employed was because the Chief Constable was — like him — a dying breed. There'd been various pressures on him to retire for some time, but he'd always kept the right side of the line and had never given anyone any ammunition to push him. In many ways, it had been a lesson in diplomacy and keeping enough people at arm's length to ensure things kept running smoothly.

Hawes hadn't been a huge fan of police restructuring and fancy office blocks, either. He'd chosen — unconventionally — to maintain an office at Mildenheath, under the pretences of keeping a watchful eye on an area of high crime, but in reality far more comfortable here than dealing with KPIs and coffee machines at Milton House.

'Jack, how's it going?' Hawes asked, his Lancashire accent still strong.

'Good, thanks. And yourself?'

'Can't complain. Can't complain. Any luck with the body in the woods?'

'Not really, sir. He's not saying much. Didn't even thank us for lunch.'

Hawes smiled. 'Customer's always right, Jack. Even if they're dead. Especially if they're dead. Have you seen the social media sites today?'

'Well, no, sir. It's not one of my daily habits, I must admit.'

'Local Facebook groups are going wild. Word's got out about Matthew Hulford, and the usual keyboard warriors are slating the police, giving us their own bizarre theories and causing general hysteria. We need to steady the ship. I'm being leant on by the PCC to make sure we get a public statement out there sharpish.'

'You want me to make a public statement for Facebook?' Jack asked.

'Not exactly, no. For all media channels. An appeal for information. There are people out there who know what happened. Okay, so a lot of them are probably fruit loops who think Matthew Hulford was killed by a 5G mast or a flu vaccine, but somewhere amongst the noise is someone who knows who killed him. We need to play up the fact he was a young lad with a bright future. Killed on his walk home after playing computer games with his friend. All facts. We can leave out the drugs stuff for now. Alright?' Hawes asked, in a tone of voice which left Jack with no alternative.

18

Jack looked at Cleo and Dale Hulford as they clung onto each other, ready to sit down in front of the Mildenheath Police insignia. It would quite likely be their first time in front of a camera, and was almost certainly not a situation they ever envisaged themselves being in.

The press conference was to be conducted without any actual press present. Jack and the Chief Constable were determined that the messaging should be tight, focusing on what they needed to know without drawing negative attention towards Matt or his family. It also meant the press wouldn't be able to ask questions, which was something they wanted to avoid — especially as they were highly likely to focus on the rumours that Matt had been somehow involved in drugs.

Jack, Cleo and Dale sat down behind the desk and waited for the police press officer, Lisa Lewkowicz, to let them know the equipment was ready and waiting.

'Okay, just a couple of things to remember,' she said,

addressing them all. 'First of all, look down the lens of the camera as much as possible. Imagine you're talking to just one person. Don't act as if you're talking to a camera, and never as if you're talking to a group. Imagine it's one person, sitting in front of you. Keep it personal. If there are things you want to read, try and use them as notes rather than a script, because it's really obvious if you're reading something scripted — especially on camera. And most of all, don't panic. It can be daunting talking to a camera, but just remember we've got all the time in the world. If you freeze or get anything wrong, we can just do it again. Absolutely no rush whatsoever, and certainly don't worry about getting it right first time. It's really not a problem if we have to do retakes.'

As Lisa spoke, Jack knew the overwhelming likelihood was that the first take would be the one that was used. The public would perfectly understand if Matt's parents were a little on edge, nervous or stressed, and it would be far more advantageous to use the first, raw take than put out anything too polished or prepared. That would only have the effect of backfiring spectacularly, making the whole exercise pointless at best, and harmful at worst.

'Anything you're not clear on or want to check before we start?' Lisa asked.

All three shook their heads. Even Jack had to admit he was far more comfortable speaking to a room of people than he was a camera, but he was about as prepared as he was ever going to be.

Jack looked at the camera and waited for Lisa's signal,

before rolling into the introduction he'd mentally prepared over the past couple of hours.

'Hello. My name's Detective Chief Inspector Jack Culverhouse, from Mildenheath CID. I'm the senior investigating officer on Operation Artisan, the investigation into the death of Matthew Hulford. Matthew was just eighteen years old when he was found dead in Mildenheath Woods. He'd been murdered. In fact, we believe he was targeted deliberately.

'On the night of his murder, Matthew had been playing video games with a friend. This was something they did often, with Matthew leaving his friend's house around ten o'clock and heading home to bed. It was something of a routine, and one he enjoyed. We believe he was ambushed on his way home, taken to Mildenheath Woods and murdered. He had no reason to go to Mildenheath Woods of his own accord, as it wasn't on his short walk home. As of yet, we don't know why or how he ended up there. But someone out there, someone watching this, does.

'His murder has caused the most unimaginable pain to his friends and family, who did not expect or deserve this to happen. Matthew's parents, Dale and Cleo, are sitting with me here today. Imagine if you will, just for a moment, what they must be feeling. How losing their only child to a senseless act of violence has changed their world forever. Imagine how you would feel if that happened to you or your family. To put things into context, I think it's important we hear from Matthew's parents about what sort of man he was.'

Jack looked across at Dale Hulford, who'd elected to speak on behalf of the pair of them, Cleo feeling unable to speak.

Dale took a deep breath, swallowed, then started to speak, his voice delicate with emotion. 'Matthew was a bright young lad. He always made us proud. He did well at school, and although he didn't yet know what he wanted to do as a career, my wife Cleo and I have no doubt that he would have excelled at whatever he chose. He was intelligent, resourceful, well-read and could turn his hand to almost anything he wanted. He was also a quiet lad, who enjoyed nothing more than spending the evenings playing computer games with friends, or catching up with the latest TV series. He wasn't someone we ever knew to court trouble, nor to get into trouble, which is why his death has come as such an unimaginable shock to us. Even finding the right words is impossible. To know that our darling son won't walk through that door again, won't sleep in his bed again, won't wear his clothes again, won't look at us, hug us or speak to us again, leaves the most painful void in our hearts and souls. Matthew was an only child. We were a close family, and without him we are nothing. As parents, as human beings, we are begging anyone who has any information which might help to please, please contact the police. You can speak to them anonymously if you wish, but please do pass on anything you have. It might seem small to you, or you might even think it won't help, but please — please — call. We'd rather ignore something that doesn't help than miss something which does, and even the smallest piece of information could help us get justice for Matthew and begin to repair the hole in our hearts.'

Dale's voice faltered just as he finished speaking, and Jack wondered if it made him a bad person that his first thoughts were how well this would play out to its intended audience. Although there were people out there who might have the knee-jerk reaction that Matthew deserved to be killed if he was involved in dealing drugs, most people tended to forget that the murdered person only ever experienced fairly brief pain. Their families — who were often entirely innocent — were the ones who had to live with a lifetime of unimaginable grief, all for the sake of someone else's daft grudge.

Jack looked at the camera and gave his closing remarks.

'As Mr Hulford said, it's often the case that the smallest, most seemingly insignificant piece of information can lead us to discover what happened. And yes, you can remain completely anonymous. You can ring Crimestoppers, or Mildenheath Police directly, and all calls will be treated with the strictest of confidence. There are people out there, watching this, who know what happened to Matthew. They might even have been involved. They may well have had perfectly good reasons for doing so. But I want them to realise that this goes far, far beyond simply harming Matthew. Matthew is no longer with us. He can't be brought back. Your coming forward will not undo what is done. But it will at least help to bring his parents, his family, his friends, that small amount of comfort in knowing that justice has been done, and allow them to begin to recover from what's happened.'

Lisa Lewkowicz raised her hand for a moment or two, then pressed a button on the camera and nodded. 'Okay,' she said, releasing a breath she'd clearly been holding for some time. 'I think we're done.'

19

Jack got home that evening with the biggest pounding headache he'd had in a long time. He didn't often feel the stresses and anxieties of grieving families, and had historically been pretty good at distancing himself and focusing on the facts of the investigation, but something about the murder of Matthew Hulford had connected with him.

He'd seen through his own experience how easily kids could become tangled up in bad crowds. His own daughter, Emily, had almost gone down that route, and in many ways her life had been changed by it. Even now, she was soon to become a teen mother, pregnant by a local lad Jack'd had run-ins with in the past, and who was himself tied up in a life of petty crime. Jack was thankful Emily was at least safe. Even though Ethan Turner had initially shown an interest and told Emily he wanted to be there for her and their baby, he'd since declared himself to be not in the slightest bit interested in the birth or life of his child. For Jack, it was bittersweet. No parent wanted their child to unwillingly become a single parent, but when the second parent was Ethan Turner, he knew he had to be thankful for small mercies.

He knew Emily would be fine. She was more than used to adapting to unusual family situations. If anything, unusual was her usual. And, in any case, she had both Jack and Chrissie to lean on, and there was no way Jack was going to let her down again.

As of now, things were stable and settled. Jack had accepted Emily's situation and resolved to make the best of it. Chrissie was spending most of her time at the house and had already pledged her support to them both. But Jack knew this was likely to be the calm before the storm. Things never got easier after the birth of a baby, and it was the sort of upheaval that tested any relationship to its limits.

'Evening,' he said to Chrissie as he walked into the kitchen, the table plastered with paperwork, above which Chrissie's head peered.

'Hey you. Good day?'

'Nope. You?'

'Nope.'

'Yet another thing we've got in common, eh?' Jack said.

Chrissie smiled. 'Sharon at work was saying there are videos of you all over social media. I presume they're dodgy and incriminating, but I haven't watched them.'

'Ah yes. They'll be the ones of me wrestling a bear to death with my bare hands before taking on six black belts in karate. You might have noticed I've got a slight cut on my lip.'

'Yes, that'll be it. How did it go? The media appeal.'

'Too early to say. Lots of calls, some patterns, but it'll take us a while to sift through the crap and the cranks.'

One of the downsides of a media appeal was the inevitable influx of weirdos who decided it was a good idea to call in and announce their suspicions that next door's dog had carried out the murder, or that they saw Elvis Presley abseiling from a UFO before stealthily committing the crime under cover of darkness. Usually, these people were easy enough to spot and caused no harm other than wasting the time of the officers who were taking those calls, but occasionally things were more sinister.

Crank calls and false information had been taken more seriously since the late 1970s, when a man began calling the police who were investigating the notorious Yorkshire Ripper. His strong north-eastern accent, which earned him the moniker Wearside Jack, had led the police to narrow down their search enormously, to a relatively small area around Sunderland — around ninety miles away from the home of the real Yorkshire Ripper, Peter Sutcliffe. Because of this, Sutcliffe had the safety to kill three more women and attack a further two. George Oldfield, the West Yorkshire Police detective who led the investigation, was subsequently plagued with ill health, suffering two heart attacks in relatively quick succession. He never got over the humiliation, and died in 1985, just four years after Sutcliffe was sentenced. It was a story which lived long in the memory of most police officers, and determining the veracity of evidence had been paramount ever since.

'Are you feeling confident, though?' Chrissie asked. It had occurred to Jack on more than one occasion that she'd never sought salacious gossip or juicy tidbits from his investigations, but instead was focused solely on how he was feeling and how it affected him.

'About as confident as we can be without a name, I suppose. Someone'll crack sooner or later, and there are a few avenues we haven't explored yet.'

'Keeping the stress levels low?'

Jack gave a wry smile. 'About as low as they ever are.'

'Way to fill me with confidence.'

'How's your stuff going?' Jack asked, nodding his head towards the mounds of paperwork.

Chrissie shrugged. 'The usual. It's never-ending. Assessments, performance indicators, reports for governors.'

'Sounds familiar. Where's Em?'

'She's upstairs. She seemed a bit tired and drained, so I said she should go to bed. She's doing well, but it's not easy for her.'

Jack murmured his agreement. He was immensely proud of how Emily was doing, but naturally worried and concerned for her.

'Actually, that leads me on to something I wanted to talk to you about,' Chrissie said. 'Nothing bad. I mean, at least I hope it won't be taken badly.'

'Well you've set it up nicely, so you might as well deliver the hammer blow now,' Jack replied.

'No, no. It's nothing like that. I was just thinking, what with Emily struggling a little bit and needing our help, and me spending more and more of my time here... I mean, I've pretty much moved in already, haven't I? Unofficially. So I just thought maybe we should make it official.'

'You mean you want to worm your way in, stake your claim to half of everything I have and leave me destitute on the streets?'

'Yep, got it in one.'

'Sounds like a great idea to me.'

Chrissie laughed. 'Seriously, though. I think some sort of structure would be really helpful for her. Everything seems so chaotic when there's a baby around, so I think at least forming a solid backbone for her will be crucial. And I won't even make you sign the house over to me.'

Jack smiled. He couldn't deny it was not only a great idea, but something he dearly wanted himself. For him, there was only one sticking point. 'I'm just worried what she'll say about it. Things are stable now. I don't want to rock the boat.'

'You've changed, Jack Culverhouse.'

'I know. I just think... I dunno. You're right, she clearly does well with the routine and knowing where things stand, but that's just it. She knows where things stand now. She's got an out. You're here, but not living here. She's got the best of both worlds. If she decides she wants you gone, it's doable.'

Chrissie shrugged. 'That's always doable. I'm not one to hang around where I'm not wanted.'

'No, I didn't mean it like that.'

'I know you didn't. But we can make it more permanent. Move my stuff in. Rent my place out. See how it goes. If it works, great. If it looks like it's causing issues, I can be back in my place pretty quickly.'

'I'm sure it won't cause issues. I just... Em and I haven't exactly had the smoothest of relationships over the years. She had a difficult upbringing and that's made stuff a bit more volatile for her. I get that. The stability helps her a lot. I just want to make sure we approach it in the right way, y'know?'

Chrissie smiled. 'I know. Trust me, I know.'

'Leave it with me,' Jack said, feeling less than certain about it himself. 'I'll speak to her.'

20

The sun rose on a frosty morning as Jack pulled his car into the car park at Mildenheath Police Station. For him, it was the perfect metaphor. As the cold and ice began to set into the ground, the investigation into the death of Matthew Hulford had started to slow down and freeze, too.

It was two weeks since the media briefing, and each of the calls they'd received had led them down a dark alley — sometimes literally. A number of the calls had referred to Matthew being involved with drugs, but it was impossible to know how many of those people had only heard that information second-hand from social media. Jack never ceased to be amazed at how often people touted hearsay and gossip as absolute fact on these platforms — as did those who read it.

As a rule, the public thought nothing of tarring someone's reputation based on a random social media post. To them, the salacious gossip and rumour was a far more tantalising and enticing prospect than any level of worry or concern as to what damage their actions would cause.

As a result, they'd fielded a number of calls from people who claimed they absolutely *knew* Matthew Hulford was involved with drugs, purely because they'd read it on Facebook. Each time something like this happened, Jack began to see how easily dictators and demagogues were able to control the political narrative and drive public opinion. As far as he was concerned, social media had a huge amount to answer for, and would not be looked upon kindly by the history books.

He'd noticed the mood and atmosphere in the incident room becoming gradually more subdued, too. In the first days of an investigation, everyone was fervently rushing around, determined to catch that early break and be the one who uncovered that crucial piece of information which would lead them to their killer. Of course, the more time went on, the more that hope and expectation was sucked out of them. It was often the way during a drawn-out investigation, and in many ways it was what sounded the death knell for many of them. As a result, cases tended to be closed once they'd exhausted their energy and resources, even though they were often opened again at a later date when new evidence came to light and that much-needed spark was provided, igniting new energy into the investigation.

Jack'd had no indication there were plans afoot to close Operation Artisan any time soon, but after many years in the job he was adept at detecting the ebbs and flows of an investigation, and at the moment it seemed as though they were in a deep lull. At times like this, break-throughs were crucial to maintaining the team's energy — both mental and physical — and ensuring the investigation didn't burn out into a slow death. And he was well aware it was his job as the senior investigating officer to keep morale up and ensure every plate stayed spinning.

He walked through into his office and sat down, looking out through the door, able to see only Wendy Knight and Ryan Mackenzie. Both were on the phone, nodding and writing down notes as they did so. He felt proud to have such a dedicated team, and silently hoped for the breakthrough they needed, which would energise them and breathe new life into Operation Artisan.

He unlocked his computer and checked his emails, finding nothing of interest. There were the usual internal emails on staff wellbeing, a couple of officers trying desperately to arrange a social gathering outside of work, energetic 'morale booster' emails from the higher-ups and a number of dark-humoured jokes and forwards. As he highlighted a few of the emails ready to drag and drop into the bin, he noticed Ryan MacKenzie putting down the phone and making her way towards his office.

He looked up as she knocked and entered, and imme-diately recognised the look on her face. It was the look of new energy, of excitement and nervous anticipation. He'd seen it many times before, and it always gave him a buzz because he knew what was coming. They'd found some-thing — something which could provide the break-through they needed.

'Sir, I just had a call from a man called Gerald Northcott, who lives on Naismith Road in Mildenheath. It's one of the roads that leads up towards the woods. He said he'd been away on holiday for three weeks, and saw the news about the murder when he got back home. He's got CCTV cameras on the front of his house, which cover the footpath and a bit of the road, too. So he checked it for the night of Matthew's murder. He says it shows two lads walking down Naismith Road in the direction of Mildenheath Woods, then a little while later we see one of them walking back in the other direction alone. We're sending officers round to retrieve the footage, but from the description he gave me over the phone, it sounds a hell of a lot like that other person might be Connor French.'

21

Jack watched with clenched teeth as the video played. The quality of the footage wasn't brilliant, but he still immediately recognised the pair. Connor French was a distinctive-looking guy at the best of times, and there was no doubt in his mind that this was who he was watching, walking alongside Matthew Hulford towards Mildenheath Woods. Walking him to his death.

'Their phones never left Connor's house,' he said, to no-one in particular.

'No,' Wendy replied. 'Which means they left them there, for some reason. Might've been to go out and do a deal? I'd imagine they're pretty clued up on phone tracking and things, so maybe they tried to play it safe.'

'Yeah, but look at this. The bit where Connor's walking back. Does he look like he knows what happens next?'

'I dunno. Difficult to say. He's walking a bit faster than

he was, but I don't know if that means anything. Probably not.'

'Looks to me like he's agitated.'

'Maybe,' Wendy said. 'But look. He's wearing a white tracksuit. Do we really think he had the awareness and forethought to make sure they both left their phones at home, but still went out in a white tracksuit to slit his friend's throat? Seems a bit risky to me, to say the least.'

'I know. But stranger things have happened. Let's get French picked up, and make sure we find that fucking tracksuit. If there's even the slightest speck of blood on it, we've got him.'

Within the hour, Connor French was being booked into the custody suite at Mildenheath Police Station. Jack watched from a back room as French gave the custody sergeant his details and answered the questions he was asked. The first thing that struck Jack was that French didn't seem to be overly concerned. Jack knew the lad had never been arrested before, but he seemed quiet — almost resigned — to what had happened and would happen. Jack knew, though, that just because someone expected to be arrested didn't necessarily mean they'd committed a crime.

He headed back to the incident room and sat with Wendy as they developed their interview strategy. The initial interview would be fairly straightforward: this was where the suspect's story would be laid out and set. Even if they knew the story to be untrue at this point, they'd still allow him to speak and let him take enough rope to hang himself. If they contradicted him and laid their cards on the table too early, he could clam up and stop talking altogether.

A short while later, they were confident they had enough to conduct their first formal interview. Up until today, Connor French had been the last confirmed person to see Matthew alive. But now he was their prime suspect.

Connor French cut a sorry figure as he sat behind the table in the interview suite, the greying duty solicitor sitting next to him. Jack and Wendy sat down, having decided in advance that Wendy would lead the interview.

'Okay, Connor. I know we've met before, but I'm Detective Sergeant Wendy Knight, and this is my colleague, Detective Chief Inspector Jack Culverhouse. I understand you've been told the reasons for your arrest?'

'Well no. I understand what the guy said, but it doesn't make any sense.'

'Okay. We can go through it in detail. The main purpose of this interview is to ascertain the sequence of events on the night Matthew Hulford died. It shouldn't be anything too taxing or difficult. Are you happy to continue?'

Connor nodded his head.

'Alright,' Wendy said. 'So let's start at the beginning. What time did Matthew arrive at your house that day?'

'I dunno exactly. A bit after six, maybe?'

'Does ten minutes past sound about right?'

'Yeah. Maybe. I dunno.'

'And how did he get to yours?'

'He walked.'

'Had he been to see anyone on the way?'

'Not that he told me.'

'And what had you planned to spend the evening doing?'

'Playing games on the PS4. Same as we always do.'

'No plans to go out anywhere?'

'No.'

'And did you end up going out anywhere?'

'No.'

'How did he seem that evening?'

'Fine. He didn't mention anything about anyone trying to kill him, if that's what you mean.'

'He wasn't nervous? On edge?'

'No.'

'Did he mention going to see anyone at all?'

'No.'

'Okay. And what time did he leave yours?'

'We've been through all this. Just after ten. Couple of minutes, if that.'

'Was he walking home again?'

'Yes.'

'Did he mention going anywhere else on the way home? To meet someone, perhaps?'

'No.'

'Did you see which way he went home?'

'No, I closed the door and that was that. I didn't think

I needed to watch after him to make sure he got home safe.'

'Was anyone else in the house?'

'No. Mum and Dad had gone down to London to see a show.'

'Might any neighbours have seen him leave?' Wendy asked, even though they'd already conducted door-to-door enquiries in the small cul-de-sac and no-one appeared to have seen a thing.

'I dunno. I haven't spoken to any of them if that's what you're asking.'

'Okay. Did Matthew often go walking in Mildenheath Woods at all?'

Connor shrugged. 'Not that I know of. Definitely not late at night when it's dark, anyway.'

'Which way would he normally walk home, do you know?'

'There's only really one way. Left at the end of my street, down Laurel Road then turn right up Hutchison Way and his road's off on the left.'

'And to get to Mildenheath Woods, he'd have to have turned right at the end of your road, then right again onto Naismith Road, is that correct?'

'Well, yeah. I mean, I can't guarantee he didn't 'cos I didn't see which way he went at the end of my road, but there's no reason why he would've gone right. Not that he told me, anyway.'

'Did you always tell each other everything?' Wendy asked.

Connor seemed to consider this for a moment. 'Well, I thought we did. Now I'm not so sure.'

Wendy looked at him and nodded slowly. She knew Connor French was lying. She knew he'd walked in the direction of Mildenheath Woods with Matthew. All she needed to find out was why.

22

Jenny sat propped up on her bed, her back against the headboard, hugging her pillow tightly. She'd never felt so alone. If she was true to herself, she'd always feared things wouldn't end well when it came to Matt, but she'd never imagined this.

At best, he'd have had a choice to make: continue with what he was doing, or pack it all in and settle down with her. He'd told her often enough that was what he'd wanted, and she felt certain he'd been about to take that leap.

She didn't want to make him choose between her and the lifestyle he was living. She hadn't needed to, either. She'd always been pretty laid back about drugs. She'd never been interested in trying them herself, but if other people wanted to then what was the problem? Her main worry was that she wanted to settle down and live a normal life, as he'd claimed he'd wanted too, and that meant Matt was going to have to change at some point.

She'd seen signs that he'd recognised that, and that he was trying to change. He'd made noises about getting a job, recognising that the longer he stayed out of the employment market, the more suspicious it was going to look and the harder he was going to find it to get a job in the future. In essence, he'd be locking himself into a life of crime. But in the next breath he'd spoken about how dealing was providing them with a good income and would set them up for life.

Matt had never been particularly into drugs. He didn't take them himself, and as far as he'd been concerned it had been a means to a financial end. Although the money had been an obvious lure for him, Jenny felt sure he would've found a way out of that lifestyle sooner or later. But it hadn't come soon enough, and now she'd lost everything.

It amazed her how much one event could shake up everything. Her parents hadn't even been massively keen on Matt, yet even they'd been hit by what'd happened. She could hear her mum and dad in the kitchen below, shouting at each other in the condescending, patronising way they did when they were stressed out. If she listened carefully, she could even hear what they were saying.

We're meant to be putting spare cash away for a rainy day, Clive!

Money. It was always about money. Money had ruined Matt, and she would be damned if it was going to ruin her parents as well. Who gave a fuck, anyway? If that was anyone's primary motivation in life, then more fool them.

Don't fucking tell me what to do. Who earns the money round here anyway?

And there it was — the Clive Blake power play. When all else failed, when the argument was already well and truly lost, his last resort was reminding everyone else who was in charge.

That was what she'd loved about Matt. He'd never played at being a big time dealer or swaggering round with a ton of attitude. Maybe that was how he'd managed to fly under the radar. And it was what had told her he'd give it all up one day. For her. For them.

It had never been anything major, anyway. Just a bit of puff here and there. And that was what didn't quite add up. Sure, people were killed over drugs all the time, but that was usually the serious stuff — Class As — in enormous quantities, and when people hadn't been paying up. Matt had only ever really dealt weed, in fairly small quantities and there'd never been any issues with the money side of things. As far as she was concerned, it didn't make any sense. Sure, he was no angel, but he always tried to do bad things the right way, and there'd never been any indication that he'd fallen out with anyone or that anyone wanted to hurt him. He wasn't a big enough player for that. Nowhere near. There had to be more to it — she knew there did.

But as much as she tried to rationalise it and make sense of it all, the overriding feeling was one of immense grief. The needless, senseless way of it all was what made it worse. Before she knew what was happening, she was crying again, her chest heaving as she pushed her face into the pillow, allowing it to absorb her sobs.

A few moments later, she heard the familiar creak of her bedroom door opening.

'You okay?' her dad said, his voice gentle and soft, a complete contrast to the argument she knew had been going on downstairs only moments earlier.

'Yeah. Great,' she replied, the pillow muffling her voice.

'Look, tensions are high for everyone at the moment. Your mum and I... We're on edge, too, after what's happened. We're worried about you. We've never had anything like this in the family before. We don't know how to deal with it any better than you do. That's why I think we need to all try to work together on this, yeah?'

Jenny nodded. She certainly couldn't disagree with that sentiment.

'How are you feeling?' he asked. 'If that's not a stupid question.'

'It's not,' Jenny said, shrugging. 'I don't know how I feel. Sometimes I feel nothing, and then all of a sudden I feel everything at once. I don't really know how to explain it.'

'It's grief,' her dad said, sitting down on the bed and putting a hand on her shoulder. 'To be honest, there's no right or wrong way to deal with it. You were only a toddler when my mum and dad died, but that was really the first time I'd had to deal with anything like that, too. I remember it being really weird, because even though I'd just had this really sudden shock, especially losing both of them at the same time, this odd bureaucratic process just sort of kicked into action. Before I'd even really had time to process what'd happened, I was being asked to sign forms for undertakers, file death certificates, organise funerals, arrange burials... It was just bizarre. And then after all that was done, the initial shock had passed and we were a couple of weeks further down the line and I don't think I ever really dealt with it properly. Everything just swings into gear and the processes take over. Every process except the grieving one, apparently. I know things are a bit different here, because you won't have to deal with all that stuff, but what I'm saying is that there's no right or wrong way to grieve. There aren't any rules. And I guess I'm also saying that even though I don't know how to deal with it either, because the only experience I have I didn't get the time or the space to deal with it, I'm probably not going to be much help in that regard. But I'm going to do my best anyway, okay? I'm here. If you want to cry, scream, laugh, whatever. Your mum and I are both here. And even if we seem to be dealing with it badly ourselves, it's not because we don't care or because we don't have the time to help you. Far from it. It's because we need help too. And we all need to help each other. Does that make any sense at all or have I just been blurting randomly?'

Jenny let out a small laugh. 'No, it does help. I just... I dunno. It doesn't feel real, you know?'

'I know. But life has it's strange ways of throwing things like this at us. It tests us. It throws us curveballs, especially when we least expect it. Everything seems to be rolling along nicely, we don't have a care in the world, then life shits on us. But that's why it's so important we all stick together.'

Jenny leaned forward and hugged her father — something she hadn't done for a long time. Not properly, anyway. And in that moment she felt — even if only slightly — that things might just turn out to be okay.

23

Jack and Wendy sat down in the interview room for the second time that day, this time feeling rather more confident than they had before, but trying not to let too much show.

They'd wondered if Connor French might've been clever enough to have anticipated their questioning and know what they knew — especially considering the questions they were asking. But he'd stuck resolutely to his guns, denying he'd ever left the house and kept to his holier than thou story. This gave them a distinct advantage, as they could prove categorically that what he'd told them in the first interview had been a pack of lies. Smarter suspects tended to stick to the truth as much as possible, changing only one or two small details to keep themselves on the side of innocence, whilst not being completely disprovable.

'Okay, Connor,' Wendy said, leading the interview, 'we spoke to you a little earlier on and asked you a few questions. I just want to run through a few of those again and make sure we're clear on the answers. You said that Matthew arrived at your house around ten past six in the evening, having walked, and that you didn't think he'd seen anyone on the way. Is that right?'

Connor considered this for a moment. 'Yeah.'

'Okay. You said he seemed fine, wasn't nervous or on edge, and that he left yours just after ten. Are we still on the right track?'

'Yeah.'

'At that point, you say he walked home and you stayed at yours.'

Connor stayed silent.

'Connor? Is that correct?'

'Yeah,' Connor replied quietly.

'Okay. DCI Culverhouse has a tablet here, with a video on it. It's a recording of some CCTV footage we've obtained from a house on Naismith Road. We'd like you to have a look at it, please.'

Jack pressed the play button and the video started. Wendy, however, was watching the faces of Connor French and his solicitor, looking for any flicker of recognition that they were well and truly fucked.

'What do you see on the video there, Connor?' Wendy asked, as Connor's solicitor leaned in to whisper into his ear.

'I dunno. You tell me.'

'Okay. I see two lads walking down Naismith Road in the direction of Mildenheath Woods. Then, later on, only one of them walks back. Do you recognise either of the lads, Connor?'

His solicitor leaned in to whisper in his ear again.

'No comment,' Connor replied.

'I think the one in the dark clothes looks a lot like Matthew.'

'No comment.'

'Isn't it a bit odd that someone who looks a lot like Matthew walked in the direction of Mildenheath Woods on the night Matthew died, but didn't come out again?'

'No comment.'

'Do you recognise the other lad, Connor?'

'No comment.'

'Because I think that one looks a lot like you.'

'No comment.'

'Do you own a white tracksuit like that?'

'No comment.'

'Okay. Because I can tell you that officers have seized a white tracksuit that looks a lot like that one from your home address. Do you want to say anything about that?'

'No comment.'

Connor's solicitor leaned back into him. After a few moments of whispering, Connor nodded and the solicitor spoke.

'Excuse me, but could I have a few minutes alone with my client please?'

24

Just under an hour later, Connor's solicitor indicated that they'd prepared a statement from Connor, which he wanted to have read out and placed on record.

'My client has made it clear to me that this is his full and final statement on the matter,' the solicitor said, sitting down next to Connor.

Jack and Wendy knew damn well that wasn't the sort of language Connor would use, and that the solicitor was trying to play hardball. They sat themselves down and listened to what he had to say, reading the prepared statement in Connor's words.

The first half of the statement covered what they already knew — the time Matthew had arrived, what they'd done and when he'd left.

'Shortly before Matt left my house,' the solicitor said, speaking Connor's words, 'he mentioned to me that he was due to meet someone about a potential deal. I don't know the person's name, but it was someone he hadn't met before, so he wanted me to come with him. I could see he was uneasy, so I agreed to walk to Mildenheath Woods with him to meet this person.

'We walked together, via Naismith Road, which is when we were captured on CCTV according to the evidence the police have in their possession. We left our mobile phones at my house, as is normal for us when we want to cover our tracks and protect our movements. When we reached Mildenheath Woods, I waited with Matt for a few minutes until his contact appeared. When I realised it was safe and Matt was comfortable, I left and walked back home the same way I'd come. As it was dark in the area and we only had moonlight and a small torch to go by, I didn't get a good look at the person Matt was meeting and cannot confirm their identity, age or any distinguishing features.'

The solicitor put the sheet of paper down on the table and looked at Jack and Wendy.

'What, is that it?' Jack said.

'That is Mr French's full and final statement.'

'Well, it's not good enough, is it? Your client,' Jack said, following the solicitor's lead in referring to Connor as if he wasn't sitting right there, 'was the last person to see Matthew Hulford alive. In fact, he's on CCTV walking him to the place of his execution, then walking back home alone. If you think some cock and bull story about a mystery man in the darkness is going to explain that away, I'd advise you to get yourself down the job centre sharpish.'

'With the greatest of respect, Detective Chief Inspector,

I don't believe you have any evidence of my client's involvement. He's already explained why he walked to Mildenheath Woods with Mr Hulford, and has given a full and frank account of what happened. He can't be held liable for something done by a complete stranger when he wasn't even there.'

'And we've only got his word for it that he wasn't. What evidence is there this mystery stranger even exists?'

'I'm afraid it's not my job to uncover evidence for you, Detective Chief Inspector. My job is to represent my client. But whilst we're on the subject of evidence, I believe you recovered the clothing my client was wearing on that night, expecting it to be blood-spattered. May I enquire as to the outcome of those tests?'

The solicitor's smug grin could've curdled milk. Jack dearly wanted to slap seven shades of shit out of it, but decided against doing so.

'Don't worry, we'll let you know as soon as we've got conclusive results,' he said, by now already knowing there were no signs of any blood spatter on the tracksuit.

More in-dept tests would be done, but with no visual indication that the pure white tracksuit had ever been stained with blood — and there would've been a lot of it — he knew it was virtually impossible for Connor French to have murdered Matthew Hulford in that tracksuit. But that didn't preclude the possibility that Connor had either deliberately led Matthew Hulford to his murder at the hands of someone else, worn a previously-stashed protective covering or even had two copies of the same tracksuit. The footage of Connor walking home only really showed him from behind, and not his front, which would've been the area likely to have received the blood spatter.

Regardless, Jack knew the custody clock was ticking, and Connor French would either need to be charged or released by the time his twenty-four hours were up. He was unlikely to even be granted an extension, never mind authorisation to charge from the Crown Prosecution Service.

Jack stood and left the room, gesturing for Wendy to follow him.

'Send the bugger back to his cell,' he said. 'There's more to it than this. A lot more. Something doesn't sit right. How long have we got?'

'Plenty, to be honest. Seventeen hours. Most of them overnight ones. Reckon you'd be able to get an extension?'

Jack scrunched up his face and shook his head. 'Unlikely. Let's face it, if it was him, he's not likely to be a threat to anyone else, is he? It's a deal gone wrong, a motive he's kept hidden from us or something else entirely. But he's no serial killer. It'd be the usual story. Keep obs on him, get his passport, report in to bail desk every few days.'

'It'd give us more time to get to the bottom of things properly.'

Jack sighed. Even though he knew Wendy was right, he hated having to open the exit door to people he strongly suspected were involved in major crimes, whether they were a threat to anyone else or not. His overriding desire for complete justice at almost all costs was something that had never left him, and in many ways he hoped it never would.

'Thoughts?' Wendy asked.

Jack sighed again. 'I think I'm going for a quick pint at the Albert, then I'm going home.'

25

Even though the Prince Albert was a pub favoured by police officers — being situated, as it was, right next to Mildenheath Police Station — business was hardly ever discussed there. There'd been occasions where Jack and his team had gone for a few drinks after work with the express intention of chewing their way through a case, but the unspoken rule was that they didn't talk shop. And that was one of the reasons Jack liked going to the Albert on his own: it meant no-one talked to him about anything.

Jack Culverhouse had very few pleasures in life, but one of them was sitting in the corner of a pub with a pint in his hand, watching the world go by as his mind gently processed his thoughts. He found it calming, almost meditative. It also allowed him to keep his finger on the pulse locally, as well as giving him a strong idea of the direction of social travel. Overhearing conversations in pubs, he found, was a great community and political indicator. Never mind polls and surveys; the boffins could simply pop down to their local and earwig on a few conversations. To Jack, there was no greater institution and social bellwether than the British pub.

Tonight, though, the Albert was relatively quiet. There were a few regulars he recognised, who'd been visiting the pub daily for as long as he could remember. He often wondered where they got the money from. Some of the beers were approaching five quid a pint, and he estimated some of these old boys must sink five to ten a day. Fifteen hundred quid a month was a fair chunk of change, especially when you didn't have enough sober hours in a day to hold down a job. Regardless, he was pretty sure the landlord didn't mind.

Jack decided he'd nursed his one pint long enough, so he sunk the dregs and walked back to his car. There were days when he'd been sorely tempted to leave the car at work, have a second pint — and more — then walk home, but it was rare for that temptation to override his aversion to physical exercise.

He arrived home a few minutes later, parked the car then headed inside. The smell of dinner cooking was a welcome one, and he gave himself a silent pat on the back for managing to make it home in time for yet another warm meal — something he'd rarely done for many years. Now, though, he had two very good reasons for doing so.

'Good day?' Chrissie asked.

'Not amazing, but we'll get there. Where's Em?'

'She's in the shower. She'll be down in a bit. Before she

is, I meant to ask you, have you given any more thought to what we talked about?'

Jack looked at her blankly. 'Come on, Chrissie. Narrow it down a bit.'

'About me moving in permanently, I mean. Making it official.'

'Christ, that was weeks ago.'

'Yes. Exactly.'

Jack sighed. 'Sorry, I haven't really had the time to think much lately.'

'You've had a fortnight. Anyway, does it really need much thinking? You must know deep down whether or not you want to make things official. I mean, I'm pretty much living here anyway. All I really need to do is move the furniture into storage and tell Royal Mail I'm here so I don't have to keep going back every couple of days to pick up my post.'

'I'll text the Postmaster General for you.'

Chrissie gave a small placating laugh. 'I think he went out with the telegram. Finger on the pulse as always, Jack. But seriously. Have you spoken to Emily about it yet?'

'Not yet.'

'You probably should. If you want it to happen, that is.'

'Course I do. I just… I haven't found the right moment yet.'

'What does the right moment look like?'

'I dunno.'

'Exactly. Look, this baby's going to be here in a few

weeks. It'd be good to have everything settled and sorted before then, no?'

'Yeah, I know. I just need to find the right time to tell Em.'

'Tell Em what?' a voice called from behind him.

Jack turned round. 'And if there was ever a time for a heavily pregnant person to get down the stairs silently for the first time ever, this had to be it, didn't it?'

Emily ignored the joke. 'Am I missing something?' she said. 'What is it you're not telling me?'

26

Jack had very much wanted to speak to Emily in his own time and his own way, but that luxury had been somewhat forced from him. Chrissie was right — it wasn't a big thing in practice, because it was virtually identical to their current arrangement. But it still felt like a big step.

Jack hadn't had a woman living with him since Helen had left, and he'd been pretty certain he wouldn't put himself in that position again. He'd been happy on his own. And, if he was honest with himself, he'd wondered if, perhaps, those times might even return again. Moving someone else in permanently would draw a line under everything. His solitude — on which he'd become quite keen — would be over, and it would also end the possibility of Helen coming back and their family life returning to normal.

And that was when he told himself: this *is* normal family life now. With Emily well into her teens, it wouldn't be the same with Helen anyway. In hindsight, they'd only ever really stayed together for Emily, and there wasn't a logical, sensible world in which Jack could ever see himself rekindling that particular tyre fire.

Perhaps drawing a line under everything and officially starting a new era was what he needed. Deep down, he knew it was. But it was still an enormous step to take, particularly at his stage of life. Then again, the coming weeks would herald in a huge new era whether he liked it or not. The arrival of Emily's baby would turn his world upside down and change things forever. Why not combine the two together and use this opportunity to start again?

These were thoughts he'd been throwing around in his mind for days and weeks, and he'd come to the growing realisation that it had simply been him being stubborn and resistant to change. There was no doubting it would be a wonderful move for them all. It just required him to lift a finger and pull the trigger, even though that seemed like the most arduous task in the world.

'Listen,' he said, sitting Emily down at the kitchen table and talking to her. 'Things are about to get a whole lot busier in the next few weeks. My work's... chaotic, to say the least. We want to make sure you've got the support you need, alright?'

'I'll be honest, Dad. That doesn't sound like something you needed to work yourself up to saying. What's the rest of it?'

Jack exhaled. 'Look, we don't want to smother you or force you into anything, and we definitely don't want to be causing you stress at the moment. Or any moment. It's going to be tough, though. Much tougher than anyone ever says or than you think it'll be. So we've been thinking of ways we can make sure you've got all the support you need, all the time.'

'Okay?'

Jack looked at his daughter, unsure as to how she would react. He hated feeling like he was walking on eggshells all the time, but he was desperate not to lose her again, and he didn't feel as though he could ever predict her reactions to anything.

'So, Chrissie and I have been talking, and it's not anything that's been decided, far from it, it's just an idea at the moment, but we've been thinking about it and looking at the options, and bearing everything in mind, we just thought that perhaps—'

'You want to move her in, don't you,' Emily said, more a statement than a question.

'Well, we just thought maybe it might—'

'Yeah, it's fine with me.'

'I mean, if you weren't comfortable then obviously we wouldn't—'

'I said it's fine.'

'Are you sure?'

Emily looked at him as if he'd just claimed the sky was orange. 'Yeah. Why, aren't you?'

'Well, yeah.'

Emily shrugged. 'There you go then. What's the problem?'

Jack blinked a few times, and realised he didn't really

know the answer to that. Before he could think of one, his phone rang in his pocket.

'Yeah?' he said, answering the call before even registering the number on the screen.

Within a minute, he was at the front door, putting his shoes on and grabbing his car keys.

27

'What the bloody hell you doing here this time of night, anyway?' Jack said as he walked into the incident room, where DC Debbie Weston was waiting for him. He desperately wanted to ask her if the reason she was working late was because her sordid affair with the land-lord of the Prince Albert had gone south, but he quickly remembered he wasn't meant to know about that.

'Working. Good job I was too, eh? It's gone off to forensics, but here are the photos.'

Jack looked at Debbie's computer screen. There was no doubting what he was looking at: a knife, which had been wrapped in plastic.

'We won't have results until tomorrow at the very earliest, but the team who recovered it reckon there are traces of dried blood where the blade meets the handle. If that matches Matt's blood, we know we've got our murder weapon.'

'Where was it found?' Jack asked.

'You won't believe it. It's a massive stroke of luck, if anything. A guy on Calderwood Street went out earlier to put a bag of rubbish in his wheelie bin. It's bin collection day tomorrow, and his bin's full, so he's gone out with his stepladder, knowing he's going to need to climb in and make some room. He lifts the lid, peers inside and sees this. I quote: "I knew it was odd straight away, because it was wrapped in a white carrier bag and I only ever use the same black bin liners."'

'Thank God for the anally retentive residents of Mildenheath.'

'Indeed.'

'Where was the bin?'

'At the end of his drive, by the footpath. He keeps it round the back usually, and had only put it out three or four hours earlier. He likes to do it before it gets dark, he says.'

'But Connor's been in a cell all day. I think we'd have noticed if he'd popped out to chuck a knife in a wheelie bin.'

'Could be an accomplice. Personally, I think the home-owner's being a bit naïve in assuming it happened on the street. It's totally possible Connor could've climbed into his garden and put it in at any point. I had a quick look on Google Maps, and his garden backs onto a public footpath and open fields. Connor could've come through the back gate or over the fence at any point.'

'Okay,' Jack said, sitting down on the edge of the desk. 'But why now? There's already been a bin collection in Mildenheath since Matt was murdered.'

'Yeah, but only a day or two after. The knife would've been too hot then. And for all our killer knows, we were checking every bin at that point.'

Jack snorted. 'Someone needs to do some research into police budgets, then.'

'Quite. But the point is, they won't have wanted to hang on to it for too long, but maybe they felt they couldn't dump it so soon after the murder either, when so many people would be out looking for it. Two weeks isn't a bad time for things to have cooled down enough for them to ditch it, without running the risk of being caught with it if they hang onto it.'

'I guess the real question is where does this leave the Connor French theory? We've searched his house from top to bottom. We'd have found a blood-stained knife, for crying out loud.'

'I know,' Debbie said. 'Which means, if it was him, he probably hid it somewhere off the property in the interim. In any case, we'll know more tomorrow. Or the day after. Until then, all we can do is wait.'

'I've spent my bloody life waiting, Debbie. We're not going to get anything before French's custody clock runs out, are we?'

Debbie shook her head. 'I'd be asking for an extension if I were you.'

Jack sighed and nodded. 'Right. I'll put a call in.'

'Okay. I'll give you a shout if anything else crops up.'

'No you won't,' Jack called from the doorway. 'Go home.'

28

Jack was woken shortly after seven o'clock the next morning by Chrissie rummaging around in the wardrobe.

'It's okay,' she said. 'Go back to sleep.'

'Bit bloody late now. What are you playing at?'

'Trying to find my other handbag. It's got my driving licence in it.'

'What do you need that for?'

'I've got to pick up the van at eight, and I need it to sign the documents.'

Jack sat up. 'What bloody van?'

'The van for picking my stuff up.'

'What, today?'

'Why not? No time like the present. It's the last day of half-term, so I'm not going to get another chance for a while. Maybe not before the baby comes. Why do you think I've been trying to get you to speak to Emily for so long? I can't just work everything around you, Jack. I've got a life and a career too. Ah. Here it is,' she said, pulling a beige handbag out from behind a shoebox. 'Christ knows what it's doing in there.'

'Well hang on a sec,' Jack said. 'You can't do a whole house move by yourself. That's ridiculous.'

'It's not a whole house move, is it? Anything I need regularly is here already, apart from a few boxes. The rest's just putting furniture and rubbish into storage, mostly.'

'You still can't do all that on your own.'

'I'm not doing it on my own. Miles and Will are helping me. I've got to meet them at the van hire place in forty-five minutes.'

'Miles? Your brother Miles?'

'No, Jack. Some random bloke I've never met called Miles. Yes, my brother.'

'Well they aren't going to be much help, are they?'

'Why not?'

'Because they're... you know.'

'Gay people can lift things too, Jack. They're allowed now.'

'That's not what I meant.'

'What did you mean then?'

'I meant they're just... Well, not very strong. That's all.'

'I hardly think I need to hire Geoff Capes to help me lift a couple of Billy bookcases into the back of a Transit, Jack. In any case, I was thinking we might all be able to have dinner together later. A celebration, perhaps.'

'Maybe,' Jack replied. 'Have to see what time I get home, though. Got a lot on.'

'Alright. I'll book us a table, and if you can be there, great. If not, we'll just talk about you behind your back and gossip about how bloody rude you are for not turning up.'

Jack laughed. 'Sounds perfect. All the more reason for me to sit in the office with a Pot Noodle.'

Chrissie walked over and kissed him on the head. 'You really do need to stop living this life of luxury and excess. It's not good for you, you know. You should bring yourself down to the level of us mere plebs.'

'I'll think about it.'

'Right. Got to dash. Have a good day, alright?'

Jack took a deep breath, then let out a huge sigh. 'I'm promising nothing,' he said.

29

Jack arrived at work shortly after eight, knowing the Chief Constable would turn up around half-past. He hoped he could talk him into an extension on Connor French's custody clock, an extra twelve hours being permissible without having to take the case to a magistrate.

He spent that half an hour pulling his case notes together, even though he'd lain awake for most of the night gathering them in his head. As far as Jack was concerned, they had their man. All they needed to do now was wait for the fingerprinting, blood and DNA results to come back from the knife and they'd be able to charge French.

He knew getting an extension from Hawes shouldn't have posed too much of a problem, but he wanted to be as prepared as he could be. Besides, if the labs were busy he might have to go in front of a magistrate to request a further extension. They'd want to know why French had to be kept in custody, and why they couldn't simply bail him. He'd argue that this was a man who was a known drug dealer and suspected killer — someone who had many criminal links. It was a game of chess, the magistrate continually trying to ensure all bases were covered, poking and prodding to ensure the chances of holding an innocent man in custody for days on end were limited.

Like much of police work, although the processes and routines were the same from case to case, one never knew how things were going to turn out until they actually happened. There were too many variables involved, especially when it came to dealing with human beings. It was that unpredictability which kept people attached to the job, which otherwise would descend into a maelstrom of mind-numbing paperwork and performance meetings.

Once he felt sure he had more than enough ammunition behind him, Jack picked up his notes and headed for Hawes's office.

'Morning, Jack,' the Chief Constable said, his Lancashire drawl always more gravelly first thing in the morning. 'What can I do you for?'

'I wanted to speak to you about Operation Artisan, sir. We've got a suspect in custody at the moment, booked in yesterday, mid morning. Late last night we had a development. A local resident found a knife hidden in his wheelie bin, wrapped in plastic. It looks as though there are traces of blood in the join between the blade and the handle, so it's been sent off for testing. Fingerprints, blood analysis, DNA. Then it'll go off to pathology to confirm and match it up as the blade that was used to kill Matthew Hulford.'

'Good. Excellent. Promising stuff. Keep me posted, won't you?'

'Yes, sir. Thing is, we're not going to get results before the custody clock runs down. Fingerprints are a possibility, but unlikely. DNA'll be two days at a minimum.'

'So you're after an extension?' Hawes asked.

'I am, sir.'

'Alright. Okay. And how sure are we that this is going to come back in our favour? I mean, what's to say it's not just a knife someone's used to chop up a bit of old steak, then chucked in the wrong bin?'

'Because,' Jack said, taking a printed photograph out of his folder and handing it to him, 'this is the knife.'

'Ah-ha,' Hawes said, looking at the picture of what could only be described as a flick knife. 'That'd have to be one hell of a piece of steak, eh?'

'You're telling me. We got very lucky, actually. The resident went out to stamp his bin down so he could fit another bag in, and that's when he noticed it. Looks as if someone's laid low for a while, then chucked it in there ready for bin day. We've got officers doing a sweep of the street looking for any houses which have CCTV on the road, but we're doubtful. Nothing visible externally, and there are only sixteen houses on the street.'

'Alright. Well, keep me posted on that. And on the fingerprinting. If we've got some good news we can put out to keep people's minds at bay that we've got the right chap behind bars, that'll go a long way to silencing all this social media nonsense about drugs gangs running wild around town. Honestly, reading some of that guff, you'd be forgiven for thinking Mildenheath was some Colombian backwater.'

'Agreed, sir. So. The extension?'

'Ah. Yes. Extension. Granted, Jack. Granted.'

30

Jack could've sworn he saw Connor French's jaw tense as he gave him the news they were going to extend his custody clock. He always liked to watch people squirm when they knew they were done for, and he found it an interesting study into Connor's mind. Was this him realising they'd found something that could prove his guilt? He certainly didn't look like a man who felt victimised or hard done by, that was for sure.

Jack had spent long enough in the job to know what would've been said between Connor and his solicitor. He knew the brief would've let Connor know about the custody clock, explained that if he was being bailed after twenty-four hours then things were going well, but if an extension was sought it tended to mean they were fairly confident of a breakthrough in the next few hours, or otherwise seriously considered Connor to be a flight risk or a danger to others.

In Jack's mind, it wasn't a bad thing for Connor to be

aware the net was closing in. More often than not, especially with first-timers and people without criminal records longer than their arms, cranking up the pressure would cause cracks to appear. That's when his job became a whole lot easier. The rising panic, the sudden falling away of the ego and bravado, the desperation to cling onto something that could get them out of there — it was all music to Jack's ears.

They'd requested fast-tracked results on the fingerprints, which would only be started once the scientific services team had clocked in at nine that morning. It wouldn't take long for any prints to be found and lifted, then checked against the police database. If anyone had handled the knife without gloves, and if the police had a record of their fingerprints through previous arrests, it'd return a match. Connor's prints were, of course, now on file, but Jack knew the imminent results wouldn't necessarily be a game changer.

If Connor had been smart enough to leave his phone at home so he wouldn't be tracked, how likely was it that he'd handle a murder weapon without gloves, then dump it in a wheelie bin round the corner from the murder scene? Jack feared the results would come back with no matches — or even no prints at all — and in his mind it all rested on the blood analysis and DNA. That would be a whole lot harder to wriggle out of, and wasn't easily rectified by wearing gloves or wiping the knife down after using it.

Jack leaned back in his chair and let his hands be warmed by the mug of coffee. He didn't like waiting for things. He'd never been particularly good at getting on with other stuff when he knew results or verdicts were about to come in. More often than not, he'd lock himself in his office, put the blinds down and nurse a cup of coffee. To keep his brain calm, he'd pick up his phone and scroll through the news, and when that became too stressful he'd turn to his sudoku app, which inevitably caused him even more frustration and resulted in the phone going back on the desk and Jack going back to the coffee machine.

He'd always admired his colleagues, who could simply put it to the backs of their minds and get on with other tasks in the meantime. That wasn't Jack. He had a tendency to let things brood, and found it impossible to empty his mind of everything going on inside it.

As the years had progressed, Jack had found it harder to let go. He knew of colleagues who cared a whole lot less now than they had when they'd started, but for Jack it was quite the opposite. It was almost as if he'd invested his whole life in the job, and for that reason it felt as if there was more to lose. If he stopped caring now, or even cared less, what would have been the point of the last few decades? He'd given his life to policing, most of it to CID and major crimes, and he wasn't about to jeopardise that now.

If he was honest with himself, that was one of the things that stung most about Frank's betrayal. The pain and emotion he'd felt after that had been multi-faceted, but he couldn't deny one of his biggest issues was that he couldn't understand *why*. Why throw a long, illustrious, proud career out of the window in your last few months? His whole life's purpose had been shattered by an act of stupidity, by chasing the pound signs rather than adhering to the principles he'd spent his life defending. And that was before even exploring the personal betrayal, collusion with Jack's nemesis and the effect it'd had on the rest of the team at Mildenheath and beyond. Had it all been worth it? No. Not in the slightest. And there was no way it could ever have been worth it. That's what Jack struggled to understand most.

When he'd seen Frank in prison, he'd felt an extraordinary range of emotions. But, most of all, he felt sorry for the man. What a waste. What a fucking waste. He looked a shell of his former self, not that he'd ever been peak specimen homosapiens at the best of times. Far from the McCann payday giving Frank a long and fruitful retirement, he'd been left with nothing, and was instead rotting in a jail cell, looking like he'd aged twenty years in the space of weeks and now had one foot in the grave. Even the standard police pension was better than that.

The team had barely spoken about Frank since, and Jack didn't know whether that was a good thing or not. On one hand, it'd probably do them some good to chew things over, get their emotions and feelings out in the open and chart a way forward as a team. But on the other, what was the fucking point?

They were words Jack had found himself thinking too often recently, and his thoughts had turned — more than once — to his own retirement. He was eligible to go, able to pick up his final salary pension and spend all his time looking after Emily and the baby. He could have holidays, learn new skills, take up golf. He hated golf, but there were days he'd happily chop off his left testicle if it meant he didn't have to sit through performance review meetings and shitty office politics, only to be kicked in the teeth at the last minute.

It certainly wasn't the first time he'd thought seriously about taking retirement, but each time he had, something had landed on him like a sign from the gods, and given him a new lease of life — for a few more hours, at least. Today, that sign revealed itself as a knock at the door.

'What,' he barked, listening as the person on the other side of the door rattled the handle, finding it locked.

Jack let out a sigh, then stood, walked over to the door and opened it. Ryan Mackenzie was standing on the other side, her face lit up.

'Sir, I think you're going to like this,' she said. 'The knife that was found on Calderwood Street? There were partial fingerprints. Looks like someone had tried to wipe them clean, but they didn't do a great job.'

'Any match?'

'Amazingly, yes. Guess who?'

31

The extension to Connor French's custody clock was due to run out late that evening, and the team were now in a position where time was on their side.

After Ryan had come to him with the results of the fingerprint analysis, Jack had made a phone call, then spent the next hour waiting for a response. When it came, it hadn't been a huge surprise.

Jack had made the executive decision not to go straight in and tell Connor what the fingerprint results from the knife had shown, but instead to try a different tactic. With the extension granted by the Chief Constable, Jack had all the time in the world to crank up the pressure on Connor French slowly, hoping to watch him squirm and crack. Simply wading in and dropping the revelation on him could cause French to clam up, so he'd decided the best approach was slowly-slowly-catchy-monkey.

Jack and Wendy sat down at the table in the interview suite, having left French and his solicitor sitting there for almost twenty minutes. If he was honest with himself, Jack was quite enjoying this.

'Okay, Connor,' Jack said, once they'd got the formalities out of the way. 'We've already spoken about your account of the evening in question. When we first interviewed you, you said you'd been at home all evening, Matthew then left yours and accidentally forgot to take his phone. On further interviewing, it was then revealed that you both left your house, deliberately leaving your phones at home so you wouldn't be tracked, and walked to Mildenheath Woods — the location where Matthew's body was later found. You were also seen on CCTV heading towards the woods with Matthew, and later returning alone. Is there anything you want to add?'

'That is what is in the notes from the previous interviews, Detective Chief Inspector,' the solicitor said. 'My client has already explained that Mr Hulford had arranged to meet a contact that evening, and that he asked my client to accompany him as a matter of safety. This indicates that Mr Hulford saw my client as a friend he could rely on, and someone who would keep him safe. Hardly indicative that he saw my client as a murderer.'

Culverhouse smiled. 'With all due respect, if everyone was able to spot a murderer that easily, there would be no murders. Connor, we had a phone call last night from a local resident who found something. Any ideas what that might be?'

'You might need to narrow it down a bit,' Connor said, in a now-rare display of arrogance, clearly emboldened by his solicitor's vague posturing.

'Alright, I will. It was something found in a wheelie bin on Calderwood Street. Does that ring any bells?'

'No.'

'Okay. Here's a photo of what was found. Do you recognise it?'

'No.'

'It looks to me very much like a knife. A flick knife, I think. Can you see the dark crusting where the blade meets the handle there? It's hard to tell from the picture, but I think that might be blood.'

The solicitor sighed. 'Are you asking or telling, Detective Chief Inspector?'

'Neither. Have you ever seen this knife before, Connor?'

'No.'

'Are you sure?'

'Yeah, I'm sure. I don't live on Calderwood Street, do I? Some geezer found a knife in a bin. So what? Doesn't have anything to do with me.'

'Okay. So you don't think the test results might come back saying yes, that is blood, and in fact it matches Matthew's?'

'I dunno, do I? I wasn't there when he died so I don't have a fucking clue what happened.'

'Do you know what blood type Matthew was, Connor?'

'How should I know?'

'He was O negative. Do you know what percentage of the population are O negative?'

'Funnily enough, no.'

'Around thirteen percent. It's the third most common blood group after O positive and A positive, but still only just over one in ten people have that blood type. Connor, I can tell you that absolutely is blood. Dried blood, but still blood. And it's O negative.'

Connor shrugged. 'So?'

'So, that's the same blood type as Matt's. The blood type only thirteen percent of the population have.'

The solicitor whispered in Connor's ear.

'I'm pretty sure your brief's telling you to go no comment, which is absolutely fine, but I just want to let you know it doesn't get you off the hook by any means. He's probably also letting you know that we can't absolutely link the knife to either you or Matt without DNA results, and that they'll be a little while yet, so we're just bluffing and hoping you'll cave in the meantime. He's right about the DNA results. They'll be back in a day or two, but that's fine because we can keep you in custody for up to four days after extensions, particularly if the evidence is starting to pile up. The blood type match is a good example. At this stage, we'd be looking at a very, very strong case for full extension while we wait for the DNA results. With a little something extra, though, we might not need to wait that long. Connor, I should let you know our experts were also able to recover a partial fingerprint from the knife. Do you know whose it might be?'

Connor's face now looked very different to the expression he'd shown them a few moments earlier. 'No comment.'

'That's fine. Because I can tell you myself. The partial print has come back with a very strong match to you, Connor. Now listen. The more you answer "no comment", the worse this is going to look for you in court. I suggest you start cooperating and have a really good think about telling us why you tried disposing of a blood-stained knife after your best mate had his throat cut open at a location you've admitted to being in.'

32

Jack couldn't deny things felt different. He didn't know how, but they did. On the face of it, not much had changed. Yes, Chrissie moving in had been made 'official', but she pretty much lived there anyway, and the move was far from irreversible: she still had her old house. Despite this, it still felt like a big step, and there was a definite sense that things had changed.

It was a feeling of commitment, of security. That was something that'd be vital for Emily in the coming weeks and months, and he was beginning to put his own worries and insecurities behind him. Too many people had told him one of his flaws was getting too comfortable in situations, and he was well aware he needed to step outside his comfort zone occasionally. It didn't mean he found the prospect any more appealing, though.

If he was completely honest, he'd have to admit he was somewhat worried about giving himself over to someone else — again. He'd invested his life and his future in Helen, and that had ended in disaster. The first sign he had of his marriage being in trouble was coming home to find a note telling him she'd left him and taken Emily with her. It was only recently that he found out Emily had been living with her grandparents — Helen's mum and dad — for all these years, just a few miles up the road.

Now, he didn't even know where Helen was. The last time he'd seen her, she was three sheets to the wind in a hospital in Denmark, Jack having received a call as her registered next of kin. For all he knew, she could be anywhere between Taunton and Timbuktu, and he didn't see any reason to give it a moment's thought. Helen had thought of nobody but herself for years, despite claiming to have made her decisions for Emily, and he didn't want her to occupy the space in Emily's brain, much less give her the opportunity to poison it.

This was an opportunity for him to move on — properly. Leaving the door open, the lights on and the bed unmade wasn't going to give him any peace. It would only leave him in a constant state of mental torture, an emotional purgatory. As much as he despised the word, he hoped this would give him some closure. After all, what other options did he have? He didn't want to be one of those daft old codgers who re-marries in their seventies or eighties, wheeling out the 'It's never too late to find love' line. Granted, it might never be too late to find love, but it was certainly past the cut-off point for maintaining an erection without chomping enough Viagra to turn your piss blue.

Jack smiled inwardly. There was nothing like a good knob gag to avert his thoughts from sappy subjects and considerations of... What was he even considering? Why had the thought of marriage later in life even crossed his mind? It wasn't something that'd come up in conversation with Chrissie — not seriously, anyway — and he wasn't entirely sure which corner of his brain that thought had come from. Either way, it was the last time he'd let Chrissie choose some shitty chick flick to watch, especially after the best part of a bottle of red wine each.

In any case, it wasn't possible. Couldn't be done. Jack, like it or not, was still married to Helen. He recalled some law about being able to declare yourself divorced *in absentia*, but he thought there had to be something like six or seven years without contact before you could do that. He'd have to read up on it. Then again, how long had it been since he'd last heard from Helen? If he was honest, it'd all started to blur a little. He'd made such an effort to cleanse it from his mind, he found it difficult to recall the details — especially after this much wine.

He rested his head back against the sofa, closed his eyes and felt the hitherto-unnoticed stinging in his eyelids beginning to recede.

33

Jack arrived at work the next day thanking a lord he didn't believe in for ibuprofen. It wasn't so much the hangover that was causing him issues, but the crick in his neck after he woke up at three o'clock in the morning, head back on the sofa, mouth wide open. Chrissie 'didn't want to wake him', and had gone up to bed herself just before midnight, leaving Jack to wake up a few hours later feeling like he'd just barely won a fight against Albert Pierrepoint.

Jack knew Connor French's solicitor would likely advise holding his counsel until it was advantageous to do otherwise. Pleading Not Guilty in court and ensuring that the Crown needed to organise an expensive and potentially lengthy trial, along with the induction of a jury, was a good way to get one's sentence reduced when the likelihood of a Guilty verdict was insurmountable, but there was no real benefit to admitting everything before then, in case the defence found a gaping loophole to prod at and prevent the case from even getting that far.

For now, Jack's main priority would be gathering further evidence, crossing the i's and dotting the t's and making sure they had an absolutely watertight case moving forward towards a decision to charge. However, even he had to admit there were a few things which didn't quite add up, which was the main reason for not yet going to the Crown Prosecution Service and asking for a recommendation to charge Connor.

The team briefing that morning was less formal than usual — not that anything was ever particularly formal at Mildenheath — and Jack listened as the team relayed some of their concerns about aspects which needed addressing or tying up.

Steve Wing leaned back on his chair, his not inconsiderable belly hanging over the front of his trousers, and Jack found himself feeling sorry for the chair's springs and tensioners.

'There's something about this which don't quite sit right with me, guv,' Steve said.

'Alright,' Jack replied. 'But I'm going to need a bit more than that.'

'It just… doesn't make sense, does it? What's the motive? They were best mates growing up, joined at the hip right up until Matt gets killed. No evidence of them falling out at any point.'

Jack considered this for a moment. 'Maybe Connor wanted it all to himself. Greed corrupts. We know that.'

'But the statement from Matt's girlfriend, Jenny, says

Matt was looking to get out of that game anyway and start with a clean slate.'

'Maybe Matt wanted out and Connor didn't like that. He saw his easy little money-spinner about to fall down and reacted badly.'

'I mean, come on. We ain't talking mafia kingpins here, are we? They don't just go popping off their mates because they want to run the empire. They're kids flogging a bit of weed. It don't stack up.'

'That's for him to tell us or not tell us, Steve,' Jack replied. 'The court's not going to worry about what motive he might or might not've had. The important thing is we can place him at the scene — he's admitted as much and is on CCTV — and we've got his prints on the knife, which we can probably assume is the murder weapon.'

'But what if it's not? We're assuming it is, but thirteen percent of people have that blood type.'

'Yeah, and only one has those fingerprints. Connor French. What are his prints doing on a bloodstained knife, eh? What are the odds?'

'We still don't know for certain, though. Plus Connor was in custody when the knife was found. It wouldn't stand up in court.'

'It's irrelevant when the knife was found. It's when it was dumped that counts, and that could easily have happened before Connor was in custody. And anyway, it doesn't need to stand up in court. What'll stand up in court is those DNA results coming back and confirming that blood *is* Matthew Hulford's. Then it's game, set and match.'

'I know what you're saying,' Wendy interjected, 'but a half-decent brief could still get him off that. Just because Connor touched that knife at some point doesn't necessarily mean he cut Matthew's throat with it. They're not finding any blood on Connor's tracksuit or trainers, either. Nothing that actually directly links back to him. I mean, we know he's fairly smart when it comes to covering his tracks, but there's no way a kid of his age can kill someone as brutally as that without leaving any sort of forensic trace. No-one could. It's not possible.'

Jack shook his head. 'No, sorry. I'm not going in for coincidence over weight of evidence, even if that evidence is mostly circumstantial at the moment. Let's look at this logically. Is it more likely that we're missing one or two pieces of crucial evidence that could put the case to bed, or that the evidence we have got is all wrong and just a massive coincidence that points to Connor French having killed Matthew Hulford?' Jack looked around the room. None of his team gave him a response, but he could tell by looking at them they weren't entirely convinced. 'Alright,' he said. 'Either way, it doesn't make a blind bit of bloody difference. We make sure the evidence we've got is watertight. We look for more. We wait for the results to come through on the tests. Whatever crackpot theories anyone's got, the to-do list remains the same. Right?'

34

Jack had been half-expecting to receive the phone call, but it had still come as something of a surprise. After everything that had happened, he took mild comfort that he could at least predict some aspects of his old friend's behaviour.

He walked in through the front doors of the prison and handed his personal belongings over at reception, before being met and taken through to see Frank. It felt strangely familiar, although he knew — hoped — this visit would end differently from the last.

Frank was sitting at the table waiting when Jack arrived, and he held eye contact with the man as he sat down and said his hellos.

'How's your arse?'

'Mostly healed now,' Frank replied.

'Never mind. They told me you wanted to see me.'

Frank sighed. 'Yeah. I've been thinking over what you said to me last time you were here.'

'I thought you might.'

'I know you did. Look, you know I want to send that cunt down for what he's done to me. To all of us. You know I do. Nothing would give me greater pleasure, Jack. But you've got to believe me when I say it's not that easy. This,' he said, pointing to his backside, 'this was just a warning. You know how it goes. You reckon this is gonna be the last of it? You don't think I'm passing my porridge through a fucking sieve before it goes anywhere near my lips? You think I don't sleep with one eye open? Fuck, Jack, I haven't slept in weeks.'

'I'll be honest with you, Frank, your bedtime routine is none of my concern right now. I think I'd be more worried if you were sleeping soundly at night after what you did.'

'I know. I know. I'm just... I'm scared, Jack.'

Jack broke eye contact and looked off towards the other side of the room. 'Yeah. Well, what do you expect.'

'I don't expect anything other than what I deserve. I know that. But it still doesn't mean I want it. Not when there's something I can do about it that'll help make this all go away.'

'What, and you deserve for it all to go away, do you?'

'No. That's not what I mean. But you were right. I can help bring McCann down. I don't expect to be thanked for it or held up as some sort of Wyatt Earp figure, but who'd you rather have rotting in here, Jack? Me or McCann?'

'Can I pay extra and get both?'

'Heh. Well, I won't be getting out for some time anyway. And it's not me I'm worried about. While I keep my mouth shut, the family's safe. I don't know how long that guarantee lasts. Until I talk, presumably.'

Jacks sighed. 'I know what you mean. And yeah, I can see you're scared. But look at it this way. Do you feel any sense of loyalty to McCann at all?'

'Fuck no.'

'Exactly. It's fear, right? Fear that he might hurt your family. And yeah, for some people who're working for him, money will be a motivator. But believe me, Frank, there's no bugger out there who's loyal to him for the sake of loyalty. You know how he treats people. How he operates. The second he's inside and doesn't have any power over them, he's done for. His minions ain't gonna be falling over themselves to help him out.'

'You don't know that.'

'I know far more about Gary McCann than most people ever will, believe you me.'

Frank leaned forward, resting his arms on the table in front of him. 'I'm scared, Jack.'

'I know. I know. Look, I can't make any promises. You know how these things work. But what if I can look into keeping the family safe?'

'How?'

'I dunno. I haven't got that far yet. There'll be something. But I'll be honest, Frank, it depends on what you've got. It has to be something that'll bring McCann down once and for all. No ifs or buts.'

'Yeah. I know. Don't worry, I know how this works. I know a thing or two about evidence thresholds. You think I didn't make sure I had an insurance policy up my sleeve the whole time? Trust me, Jack, I made damn sure I wouldn't be left high and dry. I know as well as you do what McCann's like. It was a calculated risk.'

'Yeah? And how you feeling about that calculation now?'

Frank leaned back in his chair. 'If you're asking me do I regret what I did, then yeah, course. Who wouldn't? I threw the fucking lot away, didn't I? Might as well've just started robbing banks at sixteen. Could've retired a whole lot earlier.'

'You don't need to talk like that,' Jack said.

'Yeah I do. It helps. The more I tell myself what a fucking waste it's all been, the more I realise I haven't got anything to lose. Listen, Jack. You get me those assurances the family'll be safe. That McCann'll be under lock and key and his little minions aren't gonna be causing trouble. Then I'll tell you everything I know.'

Jack looked his old friend in the eye. He'd been around long enough to know bullshit from sincerity when he saw it, and he was under no illusion that Frank Vine was telling him the truth.

'Alright,' he said, straightening his back. 'I'll see what I can do.'

35

Jack's head was pounding by the time he parked his car on the driveway that evening. He felt like it was about to explode with all the thoughts and stresses running through it. He knew he should probably drink more water — or less coffee — and that he never really gave himself enough time to switch off. But it wasn't as easy as that.

He'd never been great at switching off, and as a result he'd never practised or learned how to. Now he needed to, he had no idea where to start. He'd known a number of colleagues who'd self-medicated with alcohol — and he'd been there himself on and off — but that'd never provided him with a long-term solution. Over the years he'd just learned to deal with the stress, although he knew in reality all that did was make him a ticking time bomb, liable to explode at any moment.

He opened the front door and called inside to let Chrissie and Emily know he was home, but got no response. Then he remembered: Chrissie said she was going to go to the supermarket after work to pick up the weekly shop. He glanced at his watch. She should be home within the hour, he reckoned. Just enough time to put his feet up and watch some crap on telly, or even have a bath.

He headed upstairs to find Emily, who seemed to be spending most of her time holed up in her bedroom recently. Despite the unconventional upbringing and the heavy pregnancy, she was still a stereotypical teenager in so many ways. He knocked on her door, having learned the hard way not to just walk in unannounced.

'You there, Em?' he called, wondering for a moment if she might have gone to the supermarket with Chrissie. Almost as soon as he'd had the thought, he'd dismissed it as ridiculous. Besides which, he was sure he could hear noises. 'Em?' he called. 'Alright if I come in?'

He pulled the handle down and pushed the door open a little, just in case there was something he didn't want to see. Emily was sitting on her bed, back against the head-board, knees pulled up as close to her as her protruding belly would allow, crying.

'Em? What's up?' he said, sitting down on the bed next to her, fearing the worst. There didn't seem to be any evidence of... issues. 'What's the matter, darling?'

'Trust me. You don't want to know.'

'Are you okay? Is the... y'know. Is everything okay?'

'The baby's fine. I'm fine.'

Jack breathed a sigh of relief. 'So what's the matter?' he asked.

Emily took a few moments to compose herself before speaking. 'It's mum,' she said, eventually.

A flood of worries surged through Jack. What'd happened to Helen? Was she dead? How did he feel about this?

'What about her?' he asked, as calmly as he could.

'She texted me.'

Jack considered this for a moment, then nodded. 'Okay. Is she alright? What's the matter? Why are you upset?'

'I dunno,' she said, crying again. 'Maybe it's hormones. Maybe I just... I dunno. She just started by saying "hi" and stuff. Asking how I was. I played along for a bit. Didn't tell her about the baby or anything. I thought maybe she wanted something so I sort of strung it out to see.'

'And what happened?'

Emily unlocked her phone and handed it to Jack. 'Look for yourself.'

Jack looked at the phone and scrolled through the text messages.

The first one was from Emily:

Yeah we're OK. Dad working hard as always. What about u? X

Helen's reply was immediately below:

· · ·

Some things never change eh? :) On that note... quite a lot changed for me. Got myself clean. Starting to get life back on track. Never too late, or so they say... x

Jack thought about this for a moment. Did he believe a word of it? And what did Helen want?

He read Emily's next message:

That's good. And no... never too late. Main thing is ur happy. Where are u living at the mo? X

Reading between the lines, it seemed to Jack as though Emily was being polite, but at the same time deliberately not giving too much away about herself, instead using the opportunity to find out about her mum.

When he read Helen's reply, though, he half-wished Emily hadn't asked:

I wanted to talk to you about that. I know things haven't been great between us all over the past few years, but your nan and grandad are getting on. Don't know if you keep in touch with them after all that happened. Long story short, I'm back in Mildenheath so wanted to drop you a line. Just thought it better to tell you myself rather than you finding out by seeing me in Tescos or something! I was hoping we could meet up for coffee and a chat soon. We've got a LOT to catch up on x

• • •

'She's back?' Jack asked.

'Yeah. So she says.'

Jack put an arm round his daughter. 'How do you feel?' he asked.

Emily shrugged. 'Not best pleased. Why's she got to come back now? We're just getting things back on track. And what with... y'know...'

'Hey, it's okay. I know. I know. Is that all the messages?'

'Yeah. She only sent that about a minute before you came home. I just... I didn't know what to say back to her.'

'What do you want to say?'

Emily shrugged again. 'I dunno. I forgot you'd even given her my number. I mean, she's my mum, but I've not seen her in so long, and every time she resurfaces stuff seems to go wrong. Why's she come back anyway? She's not bothered about looking after nan and grandad for the last few years, has she? Let's face it, she wasn't even bothered about looking after her own daughter, never mind anyone else.'

Jack couldn't disagree with that, but he'd made himself an early promise not to talk Helen down in front of Emily. As she rightly said, Helen was still her mum.

A thought crossed his mind: what would he say to Chrissie? What would he say to Helen *about* Chrissie? Did he need to say anything at all? Was it even any of Helen's business? Would she try to cause trouble, see Chrissie as having taken her place? How would he even try to begin to broach that subject with either of them?

As always, Helen's timing was perfect. Chrissie had only just moved in, Emily was weeks away from giving birth and Jack was — as usual — up to his elbows at work. There was no way Helen could've known any of this, but it was typical of the way her life tended to operate itself — causing maximum destruction at the most pivotal of times in everyone else's lives. If he was honest with himself, he wanted to suggest she stay as far away from Mildenheath as possible. If there was damage to be caused, Helen would cause it — to everyone and everything, but most especially of all to herself.

And as he looked at his daughter and the effect Helen had caused without even being here, he realised her destructive forces reached further than he'd ever imagined.

36

Jack spent most of the rest of the evening in a daze. He only knew one thing: Helen would cause trouble. More often than not, that trouble was something that could be dealt with, but there was far too much at stake now. Emily was at a crucial stage in her pregnancy, and they were all — finally — happy. Jack had already lost that all once, and there was no way he was going to risk it happening again. There was no way they could hide Helen's first grand-child from her and, quite frankly, Jack knew she'd be a danger.

He knew he had to act fast. If Helen was already back, he didn't have time to waste. Legally, though, there was nothing he could do. Helen hadn't threatened any of them. She hadn't physically harmed any of them. She technically still owned half the house and was Jack's wife. His options were severely limited, but there was one thing he knew: he *had* to do something.

He stood at the bottom of the stairs for a few

moments, listening for any sounds. Emily and Chrissie had gone up to bed some time ago and would now be fast asleep, but he needed to be certain. When no noise came, he slipped his shoes on, shrugged on his jacket and let himself out as quietly as he could. He felt thankful that both Emily and Chrissie had taken to being in bed by nine most evenings, as it gave him a little time to do what he needed to do tonight.

A few minutes later, he pulled his car onto the end of the familiar driveway, before stepping out onto the gravel to press the buzzer on the gates.

'Well well well,' the voice said. 'Is this is a social visit or is it strictly business?'

'Both,' Jack replied.

'Can I see your warrant, officer?'

Jack peered at the pinhole camera on the control panel, then showed it his middle finger. A moment later, the gate began to whir and open.

By the time Jack had driven his car up the drive and parked it near the house, the front door was open and Gary McCann was standing on the threshold, smirking in his purple jumper and stone chinos.

'You still driving that old thing?' he asked Jack.

'We're aging disgracefully together. Anyone else in? Oh wait. Sorry. I forgot.'

'Very good. I see you've been brushing up on your comedy. Why don't you come inside and tell me the one about the bent copper and the petrol stations?'

Jack seethed inwardly at McCann's obsequious smile and wanted nothing more than to punch him right in the sodding face, but he couldn't. He was here for a reason. And it was far from unusual for the two of them to engage in verbal sparring whenever their paths crossed.

He followed McCann into the house, closing the door behind him.

'We're a shoes-off household, Inspector. I don't know where you've been.'

'We? You're going to have to get used to sticking with the singular, Gary.'

'Now, as much as I'm enjoying all these social niceties,' McCann said, flopping down onto a sofa, 'I'm in the middle of a pretty good Netflix series and you're rather cluttering up the place. I presume you're here for a reason and not just popping in for the great company?'

Jack ran his tongue around the inside of his mouth. 'Alright. I'll level with you, Gary. But let's drop the bollocks, alright? I'll talk to you, you talk to me.'

'We are talking, aren't we?' McCann replied, his arms raised in a mock shrug.

'I mean properly. I need you to do me a favour. A big one.'

McCann's smile spread and gradually turned into a laugh. 'You want me to do you a favour?'

'Don't worry,' Jack said quietly. 'It works both ways.'

'Does it indeed? And how'd you work that out? What favours do you think I need from you, exactly? Because I'll be quite honest with you, Jack, there's nothing that springs to mind.'

Jack thought for a moment. He needed to be extremely

careful in approaching this. 'We being straight with each other?' he asked. 'Properly, I mean.'

'You tell me what you've got and what you want, and I'll let you know.'

Jack sighed. 'Alright. You've given us the runaround for a long time, Gary. You know what you're doing. Unfortunately, so do we.' It wasn't often that Jack deliberately lied to get what he wanted, but right now he had no choice. Besides which, he was quite sure there were at least a couple of disgruntled goons amongst McCann's mob.

'Pop the cuffs on then, Inspector,' McCann replied, holding out his hands. 'Or is this another load of bluff and bluster?'

'I'm always straight with you, Gary. Credit where credit's due. Don't forget, a lot of this is out of our hands now. The investigation into Frank's gone external. But the investigation into you hasn't. Now, that information all needs to match up. If it doesn't... Well, it weakens the investigation, doesn't it?'

McCann shook his head slowly. 'I'm not buying this. One of your longest-serving colleagues goes down for corruption, nearly bringing your whole team with him, and your response is to do exactly the same thing? Don't give me that, Jack. What are you playing at here, eh?'

Jack shrugged. 'It's all I've got. And, let's face it, it's all you've got too. We're coming to the end of the road here, Gary. And your tarmac's running out a lot faster than mine is.'

'Then why is it you, sitting here in my living room,

offering to lose this mystical, magical evidence you think could push me over the edge? 'Cos I'll be honest with you, Jack, I'm listening, but nothing I'm hearing's making much sense.'

Jack looked at the floor, sighed, then looked back up at McCann. 'Helen's back,' he said. 'In Mildenheath.'

McCann nodded slowly. 'And you don't want her cocking up your relationship with the new bird... What's her name again?'

'Chrissie.'

'That's the one.'

'There's more to it than that. She... Look, you and I aren't ever going to be best mates. I mean, if it weren't for our jobs then who knows, but there's a level of mutual respect there. With Helen, it's just... She's poisonous. Dangerous. Listen, Gary. Can I trust you?'

'Nope.'

'My daughter. She's pregnant. The baby's due in the next few weeks. She's been really struggling with it all. Her childhood was an absolute clusterfuck because of me. And Helen. All I want to do is put that right. Stability. A proper start for her baby. A decent family unit. Beneath all the bullshit, I'm pretty sure we agree on those principles, right?'

'I'm listening.'

'I can't let her ruin all our lives again, Gary. I can't let that happen. I'd far rather have ten of you running around Mildenheath than one of her.'

'You want her gone.'

'I'm not asking you to do anything. I'm letting you know the situation. The rest's up to you.'

'Only if I believe what you're telling me about your side of the bargain.'

'I've always been straight with you, Gary. I'm putting my fucking bollocks on the line even coming here tonight. I've got far more to lose than you have. And I can tell you now, the net's closing in on you big time. Believe me, there's nothing I want more than to see you rotting in a prison cell somewhere. Apart from one thing. The only thing I'd happily trade that for. My family.'

McCann seemed to chew this over for a few moments. 'I've known you a long time, Jack.'

'I know. I'm feeling every second, trust me.'

'Where's she staying?'

'I can get details.'

McCann looked at him and slowly nodded. 'Alright,' he said. 'Get them to me. I'll see what I can do.'

37

Almost as soon as McCann had given his answer, Jack regretted ever going to him. It had been a frantic decision made on the spur of the moment in a desperate attempt to save his family.

McCann, though, had seemed to take it seriously. There'd always been a mutual respect between the two of them, despite the deep, visceral need to get one over on each other. If Jack was honest with himself, as much as he wanted to nail McCann and watch him rot in prison, he knew that would signal the beginning of his own personal rot. The thought of finally catching McCann and sending him down had kept him going for so many years, a part of him was afraid of what'd happen when he won. What would be the point, then?

These were only afterthoughts for Jack — attempts at justifying what had already been done. His reasons for doing so had been solely to keep Helen away and protect his family.

What would McCann do? They hadn't covered that. All Jack knew was that Helen needed to be kept away, and he had no power to do so. She was his wife. She owned half their house. She'd committed no crimes. She had every legal right to return and wreak as much havoc as she wanted. But what if he... He wouldn't, would he?

In Jack's mind, McCann would simply pay her off, slip her a bit of cash and suggest she stayed away. Would Helen fall for that? How much would she need to not be near her parents in their final days? And, more to the point, how much did Gary McCann value his freedom? What price would he put on staying out of prison? And what if Helen refused?

It didn't bear thinking about. Jack knew — but had never been able to prove — that McCann had personally overseen the disappearance of people before. It wasn't a step he took lightly, but it was certainly a weapon in the arsenal for when it was needed. Would McCann go that far? And if he did, would it be traced back to Jack? No-one had ever found a single one of McCann's victims yet — and god knows they'd tried — but Jack'd put money on this one being the first. It'd be almost poetic. Inevitable.

But he knew he couldn't think like that. It wasn't helping anyone, least of all him. There was nothing to say that was the route McCann would go down. And, even if he did, what was worse: the vague, small possibility of being charged with conspiracy to murder or the absolutely certain risk of Helen ruining his entire life and happiness? There wasn't even a decision to be made.

Jack hadn't slept any better that night, and he felt the full weight of last night's events as he headed into work. When he arrived, a gleaming, grinning Debbie Weston knocked on his door.

'Perfect timing, sir,' she said, clearly struggling to hold in whatever good news she had for him. 'They're like buses, aren't they? Sit around waiting ages for one, then they all turn up at once.'

Jack sighed and scratched his head. 'Sorry, Debbie, you're going to need to explain that one to me.'

'At a bus stop, I mean. It's an old saying. You sit around waiting for a bus and none come, then three all come along at the same time.'

'For Christ's sake, enough with the buses. You haven't come in here to talk to me about buses, have you?'

'Well, no, but you asked.'

'I asked what you were referring to. What's all come in at once?'

'The DNA results,' Debbie replied, sitting down. 'The clothing's all clear. We can't say for definite those were the clothes Connor French was wearing that night. It's possible he had more than one version of the same outfit. I've got this green dress at home. Well, actually, I've got three of them. It does happen.'

'Right.'

'But there's no blood spatters on them anywhere. Connor's clothes, I mean. Not my green dresses. But, get this. There are traces of mud on the trainers which match the makeup of the mud at Mildenheath Woods, so we can safely say he wore those trainers there. Just not necessarily that night. People from all over town go walking in there all the time, so we can't say for definite the mud was picked up on the night Matthew Hulford died.'

'So we've got nothing?'

'Oh no, I wouldn't say that. The results from the blood on the knife came back, too. It's Matthew Hulford's blood.'

38

Jack knew the constant drip-drip of information and evidence would cause Connor to break at some point. They had enough to charge, he was sure of it. There was CCTV evidence of Connor walking Matthew to the woods and then returning alone. He'd admitted as much, too. Then there was the murder weapon — the knife — with Connor's fingerprints on the handle and Matthew's dried blood on the blade.

The lack of DNA evidence on the tracksuit was easily explained away by Connor owning two identical sets of clothing and, in any case, absence of evidence was not the same as evidence of absence. It was time to increase the pressure.

With the interview formalities out of the way, Jack let Wendy lead the proceedings.

'I don't think we need to spend too much time going over old ground, Connor,' she said. 'So let's assume we believe your story up until the point Matthew meets his contact, you leave him to it and head home alone. Let's say the two of you arrive in the woods. Do you want to have a little think and run me through what happened after that?'

Connor sat with his arms crossed over his chest. 'I've told you. I don't need to think about it. I've told you what happened. We waited a few minutes, the bloke turned up, I went home.'

'What did he look like?'

'I dunno. Medium height. Medium build.'

'Hair?'

'He had a cap on.'

'Colour?'

'Black. Black top, black trousers, black shoes. Barely saw the bloke. Don't think he wanted to be seen. If he did, he wouldn't be arranging meetings in the middle of the bloody woods at night, would he?'

'Do you know his name?' Wendy watched as a flicker of something crossed Connor's face. It was clear to her that he knew more about the man's identity than he was willing to let on. 'Connor?'

'No.'

'I'll give you the opportunity to think about that again. And bear in mind we only conduct additional interviews as and when new evidence comes to light.'

Connor looked at her for a few moments. 'Sam. Matt said his name was Sam.'

'Sam what?'

'I dunno. Just Sam. That's all he told me.'

'Did he tell anyone else?'

Connor shook his head. 'I doubt it. When he got there, Sam said he didn't feel comfortable with me being there too, so I left them to it.'

'Did he have an accent?'

'No, just normal.'

'And you felt happy leaving your friend with someone you'd never met, in the middle of woods, in the middle of the night?'

Connor shrugged. 'Yeah. He seemed alright. I didn't get any bad vibes. Anyway, Matt was fine with it and told me to head home. Some people don't like talking business if you turn up mob handed. It's all based on mutual respect.'

It seemed to Wendy as though Connor might be telling the truth. There was only one way to find out for certain.

'Connor, last time we spoke to you, we told you a knife had been discovered with your fingerprints on it. You didn't have an explanation for that at the time. Do you have one now?'

'I dunno. Maybe it's one my mum threw out or something. Or maybe I found it somewhere and picked it up and put it in the bin.'

'Did you?'

Connor shrugged. 'Don't remember.'

The solicitor leaned forward. 'Might I remind you, Detective Sergeant, that the burden of proof is on you to ascertain that the knife did indeed belong to my client.'

'Handling of a murder weapon doesn't require ownership,' Wendy replied. 'And the fingerprint is proof of handling.'

'Partial fingerprint. And there's no evidence it *is* the murder weapon. It's simply a knife with some dried blood on it. My client's already told you it's quite possible he found the knife whilst out walking, saw it could be dangerous in the wrong hands, so picked it up and disposed of it like a responsible citizen.'

'True, that is possible,' Wendy said, playing along for just a moment. 'But then there's the little problem of the blood itself. See, the DNA results have come back, Connor. We know whose blood's on the knife. Do you want to tell us anything?'

'What's the point? If you reckon you know, what does it matter what I say?'

'Okay. Connor, do you want to tell us how Matthew's blood got on a knife you'd been handling?'

39

The atmosphere in the incident room was tense, but expectant.

'So he just no-commented his way through everything?' Ryan asked.

Wendy nodded. 'Yep. Soon as we confirmed it was Matthew's blood, that was it. Complete shutdown. No admission, nothing. He just stopped cooperating. Not that he was ever particularly cooperating in the first place.'

'We've got enough to charge, though, surely?'

'Oh yeah. Without a doubt.'

'But?'

'Nothing.'

'She's got a "hunch",' Culverhouse said, complete with air quotes.

'No, I just think there's more to it than that. Think about it. He's smart enough to leave his and Matthew's phones at home so they don't get tracked, but has no worries about being seen on CCTV. We're claiming he's doubled up on outfits and disposed of the one he wore to murder Matthew, despite that meaning he must've had his change of clothes waiting for him somewhere in the woods. But after all that forethought and planning ahead, he handles the murder weapon without gloves. And where's the clothing? So he can dispose of an entire outfit and shoes without trace, yet the knife turns up in a bin round the corner, complete with fingerprints? I'm not buying it. It doesn't add up.'

'Maybe he got desperate,' Steve offered. 'He didn't mean to kill him. Argument got out of hand. That explains why he wasn't wearing gloves and got desperate trying to dispose of the knife.'

'That doesn't explain the clothes, though. Whichever way we try to spin this, there's nothing that means everything makes sense. There's always a huge but. We're missing something. If you ask me, I think there *was* a third person. Maybe Connor supplied the weapon. Unknowingly, perhaps. Maybe this third person's trying to frame him. I don't know. I'm not even sure Connor does know who the person is, but I don't doubt that aspect of his story. It means a lot of the disjointed stuff suddenly starts to makes sense.'

'It'd certainly explain the lack of blood on his clothing. Particularly if he wasn't actually there when Matthew was killed,' Ryan offered.

'Exactly. The mud on the shoes, too. We know he was there. He's not denying that. The only thing that leads us to think he actually did it is the knife. Yes, Matthew's blood's on it. Yes, Connor's fingerprint is on it. But

Connor could easily have handled it before or after it was used to kill Matthew. I'm just not falling for him being so forensically aware and careful about everything else, then dumping the murder weapon on top of a wheeliebin, complete with fingerprints and blood. It doesn't fit with what we know of him.'

'Then we have to work the angle that he *does* know who did it,' Jack said. 'A plea bargain, perhaps. A smart brief will be able to argue that Connor could've had no reasonable foresight that this person wanted to murder Matthew. That gets him off being an accomplice. Granted, it doesn't explain the knife situation, but that's for them to hammer out in court. If it gets us a name, I think that's an angle that should be played.'

'And if he doesn't know the name of the person?' Wendy asked.

'Then it gets a whole lot more difficult. But it all comes back to the first theory, doesn't it? It's got to be drugs-related somehow. There's no sign of the girlfriend being involved with anyone else, so we can probably rule that one out. Matthew and Connor didn't do anything much other than play video games and flog a bit of weed, so there's no real opportunity to develop enemies who want to kill you. Maybe it was a deal gone wrong. Perhaps Connor's telling the truth about Matthew going to meet a potential business associate. Maybe there was a disagreement. The person could be seriously unhinged for all we know. Off his nut on whatever substance. Either way, if Connor wants to ever see the outside world again, he's gonna have to start playing ball.'

A knock at the door interrupted them.

'Come in,' Jack barked, watching as a young PC entered the room.

'Sir, there are two people downstairs who'd like to speak with you.'

'Well I'm busy. Tell them to make an appointment.'

'Uh. Sir?'

'What?'

'It's Connor French's parents. They said they think they might have something that'll help you.'

40

As they sat in a side room explaining what had happened, the thing that struck Jack most about Connor French's parents is that they seemed far more conscience-stricken and remorseful than their son had at any point.

'I've got to be honest with you,' the mother said. 'We actually found it a couple of days ago, and we knew straight away there wouldn't be an innocent explanation. But we just couldn't bring ourselves to... you know.'

'Of course,' Jack said. 'Your instinct is to protect your child. I get that.'

'To an extent. I mean, there are limits. As we're now realising. It's just such a horrible situation. We feel guilty towards you for not telling you earlier, guilty towards Connor for telling you at all, horrible at the thought it might reveal something that gets him in trouble, even worse at the thought that a family might not get closure on what happened to their loved one if we kept quiet. It's just... There's no pleasant way out of this.'

'No. No, you've done the right thing. Is this it here?' Jack asked, pointing to the small key Connor's dad was dangling off his forefinger.

'Yes,' he replied. 'I found it in the shed. I've got a bunch of old keys hanging on a nail just inside the door. One for the garage, a spare one for the house. Probably about four or five old houses, in fact. My parents' house. They've been dead fifteen years. Padlocks. Bike locks. Windows. Christ knows what most of them are. Keys just accumulate. I might not know what they're for half the time, but I damn well know what's there, and this one stood out to me like a sore thumb.'

'To be fair, it is bright yellow.'

'That too. I reckon it's for that storage place down on the Harrington Road.'

'Well, it does have their logo on it.'

'True.'

'Have you called them? Or been down there?'

Connor's father shook his head. 'No. To be honest, we were more worried about what we might find.'

'And have you ever used this storage company before?'

'No.'

'Any other ideas as to how the key might've got there?'

'No. None at all. The only people who have access is the two of us and Connor. It has to be something bad, doesn't it? Why else would he hire a storage unit without saying anything? It's obviously something he couldn't hide around the house, or which he thought you might come looking for. I mean, he couldn't even risk leaving the key in the house, could he? Bloody good hiding place, to be fair, but he didn't reckon on me having as keen an eye as I have.'

'Or finally going out to tidy the shed,' his wife added.

'And Connor never mentioned anything about a storage unit to you?' Jack asked.

'No. Nothing.'

'Okay. Well, you've done the right thing. We'll speak to the company. We'll double check who the unit is registered to, and if there's anything in there of any use, we'll make sure you're the first to know.'

Connor's parents nodded and thanked him, before heading towards the exit. Jack looked down at the key in his hand, and wondered if perhaps it held an even more symbolic significance than he thought.

41

It would have been perfectly reasonable and normal for him to have sent someone else to check out the storage unit, but Jack was keen to see it for himself. He'd come far enough in this case, and wanted to stay as hands-on as possible.

He and Wendy parked up in the bays outside, and Jack wondered if this was the same unit where Chrissie had moved her furniture and old belongings when she moved in permanently with him.

Although getting to the car park had been easy enough, the building itself looked more like Fort Knox, with a sliding door to the reception area the only way in. Beyond that, keypad entry was required to access the storage areas themselves.

Jack and Wendy headed to the reception area, where they were greeted by a middle-aged woman in a bright yellow body warmer.

'Hello, can I help?' she said, smiling.

Jack and Wendy showed her their police ID cards. 'I'm Detective Chief Inspector Jack Culverhouse, and this is my colleague Detective Sergeant Wendy Knight. We found a key during a recent search, which we think belongs to one of your units. We were wondering if we might be able to take a look, please.'

'Ah. I'm afraid that's beyond my powers. Only the registered person on record can access the unit, unless you've got a warrant to search it.'

Jack sighed. 'Listen, we can get a warrant. That's not an issue. But it's not something that can be done instantly. It takes time, and we don't have time. Our suspect's custody clock is running down fast, and we think there could be crucial evidence in that unit. If we don't get in, he gets out and he's left roaming the streets.'

'I understand your problem. I really do. But I can't go against company policy. Not unless we know there's something illegal in there, or you have a warrant to search the unit.'

Jack leaned in slightly. 'I want to tell you something. Something I shouldn't tell you. Something that puts my job on the line, but which I think would help. And I hope you'll be able to do the same for me in return. The guy we're talking about? He's in for murder. We think he killed a young lad, barely out of college, who had his whole life ahead of him. If we don't get inside that unit and find what we're looking for, he'll be walking the streets within hours.'

The woman swallowed and looked down for a

moment, before raising her eyes to meet Jack's again. 'Is this the body they found in the woods?'

'I can't tell you that.'

'I remember reading about it. My son's the same age. Can I see the key?'

Jack handed it to her. She looked at it, then typed the serial number into her computer.

'Okay. It's a ten square footer. Our smallest type of unit. I hope you're not expecting to find a missing yacht.'

'I'll be honest, I don't know what we're expecting to find. Can you tell us who the unit's registered to?'

'A Mr Connor French.'

'Okay. What do people need to bring to hire a unit, in terms of proof of ID?'

'A driving licence usually does the trick, plus proof of address. Mobile phone bill, council tax, something like that. Or a passport and driving licence if they don't have those.'

'If they were too young to have council tax bills, for example?'

'Exactly that.'

'Okay. Can we see the unit please?'

'Follow me,' the woman said quietly, gesturing for them to walk behind the reception desk and through the office.

They made their way through the corridors towards the area that contained the storage units. When they eventually reached the unit, the woman put the key into the lock and turned it. They listened as it clicked open, and the metal door yielded.

As the door opened, it revealed a single, solitary carrier bag on the floor.

'Is that what you were expecting to find?' the woman asked.

Jack sniffed the air. 'Well it's not a forgotten egg and cress sandwich, which is a relief.' He bent down and peeled the carrier bag back, exposing its contents. It was immediately clear what they were looking at. Cash. A lot of it.

Back in the incident room, Jack briefed the team on what they'd found.

'Twenty-five grand, by the looks of things. In mostly new notes. We've got officers going through them at the moment, but from first glance it looks like a lot of them have their serial numbers in sequential order. That tells me they've been drawn straight out of the bank and taken there.'

'Or nicked from the bank,' Steve said, chuckling to himself.

'I think we'd probably have been made aware if there'd been a bank raid, Steve. Now, this doesn't look like drug money to me. There's too much, and the notes are all crisp and in sequence. That's not how it's done. No-one draws a couple of grand in fresh notes out of the bank and spends it on weed. You'd need a fucking JCB to get it home, for a start. This looks to me like blood money.'

'What, you think Connor was paid to kill Matthew?' Ryan Mackenzie asked.

'That's where my mind went, yes. Some of the notes are old and used, but most of them aren't. Early indications are that there're twelve different series of decent sizes, so we're potentially looking at at least twelve original sets of cash, plus all the loose stuff that's in there as well. We're in the process of getting in contact with the banks to see if any of them can confirm the serial numbers have passed through their hands recently, or been given out by them.'

'Back to the waiting game then, eh?'

Jack sighed. 'Yep. Looks like it.'

A couple of minutes later, Jack sat down in his office and massaged his temples. Things seemed to be getting close to a conclusion; there was a definite tension in the air, not to mention the sides of his head.

He felt confident the banks would come back with something. It was rare for a paper trail not to lead to the guilty party in one way or another. The only exceptions were when sophisticated international gangs were involved, but that could hardly apply to Matthew Hulford peddling weed in Mildenheath. Either way, all they could do now was wait for the call.

As he considered this, he heard the familiar *ping* of an email landing in his inbox. He took his phone out of his pocket and looked at the notification. It was from an email address he didn't recognise, but that wasn't what concerned him; it was the subject line that stood out most.

Are you watching, Jack?

He opened the email, which consisted simply of a Vimeo link a note:

Password: mildenheath

He was aware of Vimeo — a similar sort of site to YouTube, as far as he could work out — but he wasn't going to risk clicking any links. He jotted the website address down on a piece of paper, then opened his phone's web browser and typed in the address manually, to make sure he was actually going to Vimeo and not elsewhere.

The password box appeared, and he entered the word *mildenheath*, all in lower case as the email had styled it. Then a video appeared and started to play.

Jack turned his phone on its side to get a full-screen view, and turned the volume up. It appeared to be a restaurant scene, and the only noise was that of diners talking, cutlery clanging and the occasional door opening and closing.

It looked as though it'd been filmed on someone's mobile phone or portable camera. The shot was steady — perhaps the camera had been propped up against a salt cellar or something — and the picture quality was decent, although the sound suffered.

He didn't recognise the restaurant; it was far too swanky and pretentious for him. He was fairly sure it wasn't in Mildenheath, so he had no idea why he'd been sent the video or why the password to view it was *mildenheath*. But as the camera closed in on one particular pair of diners a few tables away, Jack realised he recognised them both.

It took him a moment to realise what was happening. They were out of context. He'd never seen them together before. And he hadn't seen her in years. She looked different. Better.

A bolt shot through him as his consciousness recognised what he was watching: Gary McCann and Helen, sitting at the same table.

It was an odd way for him to try and convince her she needed to disappear, but Jack immediately realised it was preferable to him killing her. Or was he just trying to win her trust first? Maybe he was showing her how much money and influence he had, before handing her a cheque and telling her to piss off. Jack tried to run through as many feasible possibilities as he could, but he quickly realised why. It didn't seem right. The body language was all wrong. They seemed… familiar.

Jack narrowed his eyes as his brain tried to compute what he was seeing, but within seconds there was no doubting it. He watched as McCann and Helen leaned in towards each other and held a long kiss. Moments later, Helen smiled and went back to her food. McCann, though, slowly turned his head towards the camera, giving his trademark smile and wink, especially for Jack.

43

Jack sat in near-silence, listening to the throbbing of blood in his eardrums. What the fuck was McCann playing at? He could only assume — had to assume — this was his way of currying favour with Helen and winning her trust, all while having a little dig at Jack. McCann wanted him to rise to it, but Jack knew he couldn't.

There was no reason for the video. Simply finding out a few days later that Helen was gone and wouldn't be coming back would be more than good enough for him. He didn't need 'progress updates' or evidence. He knew — thought — that if nothing else, McCann was good for his word. So why had he sent him this, if not to tease him and wind him up?

He felt annoyed, too, that it'd worked. He shouldn't give a shit if Helen was kissing someone else. They were ancient history. Yet it bothered him. And what bothered him most was *who* she was kissing.

Before he could collect his thoughts and try to force

himself to think calmly, clearly and rationally, there was a knock at his office door.

'What?' he barked.

Wendy opened the door and stepped inside. 'Good news,' she said. 'We've heard back from two of the banks already. They've confirmed that many of the banknote serial numbers we sent them were given out by them in cash withdrawals over the last couple of months. All in-branch withdrawals, ranging from one thousand to five thousand pounds at a time.'

'Right. Okay. So, uh, what else do we know?'

'Well, we know who withdrew those amounts. It was the same person each time. Both banks have confirmed that independently. And it strengthens the case against Connor French. It proves who gave twenty-five grand in cash to him.'

Jack looked at Wendy, trying to process the words she was saying. 'What? Who?'

'Clive Blake. Jenny's dad.'

'He was the one who withdrew the cash?'

'Yep. All the notes they can trace and confirm were given out by them, he withdrew. Why did he pay Connor French twenty-five grand in cash, using withdrawals he'd tried to keep under the radar?'

Jack nodded slowly as the pieces fell into place. 'Because he needed to buy his silence.'

'Exactly. His daughter was going out with a drug dealer. She was besotted with him. Talking about starting a life together. There was no way she was going to leave Matthew. So Matthew had to leave her.'

Jack tried to focus, tried to ignore what he'd just seen on that video. 'He killed Matthew to protect his daughter.'

'I reckon so. Are you happy for us to send officers round to arrest him?'

'Uh. Yeah. Yeah, makes sense. Let's do it.'

'Alright. I'll put the call out. In the meantime, we should call a briefing. Update everyone. Put a strategy together for Clive Blake's interview. We need to interview Connor, too. There's a lifeline for him here if he helps us. He could avoid a murder charge if he confirms Clive paid him off to keep him quiet. A smart brief could even claim coercion.'

'Yeah. Yeah. Good idea.'

Wendy looked at him. 'Shall I tell the others there'll be a briefing in, say, half an hour?'

Jack cleared his throat and stood up. 'Uh, no. No, let's make it a bit later. I've got to pop out.'

'Okay. What time?'

'I'll let you know,' he said, heading for the door. 'There's something I need to do first.'

44

Jack was running on pure adrenaline as he drove, a thousand thoughts flooding through his mind at once. A small voice told him he'd acted on impulse too often recently and that he should stop and think for a moment, but it was drowned out by the sheer rage and desperation taking over his body and mind.

He pulled up at the gates of Gary McCann's house and held his hand down on the horn. A few seconds later, the gate whirred and started to open.

Jack took his hand off the horn, waited for the gates to open wider, then accelerated up the driveway, crunching to a halt on the gravel outside the house. He got out of the car and marched over to the front door, watching it open just as Jack reached the steps. McCann's head was cocked to one side as he spoke.

'Everything alright, Detective Inspector? You look a little flustered.'

Jack ignored McCann's trademark and deliberate barb

in mistaking his rank, and instead asked his own question. 'What the fuck are you playing at, McCann?'

'I was having a rather pleasant afternoon with a cup of tea and a good book, if you must know. It doesn't look as though your day's been quite as relaxing, though. Is something the matter?'

'You know damn well what's the matter, Gary. What the fuck was that video all about, eh? You think you can wind me up with shit like that?'

'Well it seems to have done the trick, don't you think?'

Jack made to launch himself at McCann, but managed to stop himself.

'Oh come on now, Jack. That's a bit beneath you, isn't it? It's certainly beneath me. I'm not about to fight you on my doorstep.'

'Explain yourself,' Jack said. 'What's it all about?'

McCann sighed. 'It's called gaining trust.'

'Whose?'

'Hers. You catch more flies with honey than you do with vinegar, believe me. She wasn't difficult to find. So I thought I'd try to impress, win her round, then we can talk business.'

'That's bollocks. Why the kiss?'

McCann shrugged. 'Why not? She's a single woman. I'm a single man. It's been a while. Like I said, gaining trust.'

'You smirked at the camera, Gary. I'm not stupid. It's a wind-up, isn't it?'

'There's no wind-up at all. I can guarantee you, I'm deadly serious.'

'You're not trying to make a move on her, are you Gary?' Jack asked, his voice almost a whisper, the tone more a statement than a question.

'Strictly business, like I already told you.'

There wasn't much more Jack could do. Just as he was about to turn and leave, he heard a clatter in the kitchen. He looked up at McCann.

'Cat knocked something over,' McCann said.

'You haven't got a cat.'

'Must've been the giraffe then.'

Jack ignored the comment and, before McCann realised what was happening, he'd barged past and into the house, heading straight for the kitchen. When he got there, he found Helen standing in the middle of the room, staring straight at him.

Jack nodded slowly. 'I see. Very good. Very good. And how long's this been planned for, eh?'

'You don't know what you're talking about, Jack,' Helen said, the first words Jack had heard from her in years.

'I know what I can fucking see. So he's won you over by flashing the cash, has he? Some things never change. A bloke pulls out a wad of fifties and you turn into his little lapdog. You've landed right on your feet there, haven't you?'

Helen scowled at him. 'Fuck off, Jack. Just fuck off. Look at you. You're pathetic, running over here, snivelling like a little schoolboy. What did you think was going to happen? Did you think he was going to drive me out to the middle of nowhere and put a bullet through my head?'

Jack turned to McCann. 'You told her. You fucking told her. We had a deal. You said you were a man of your word.'

'And you should know by now that I'm not on your side, *Detective Inspector*.' McCann almost spat the last two words with venom. 'Oh, and about that deal. Deals have to be two-sided, you know, or they're not deals. Both sides need leverage. Just out of interest, what made you think you had leverage?'

'What are you talking about?'

'Ah come on, Jack. You're a clever boy. What gave you the impression that anything anyone said would reach the right ears? I knew you were bullshitting from the moment you knocked on my door. You never had any leverage. What on earth ever made you think Frank was safe in that place?'

Jack could hear McCann talking, but it was all noise. His mind was filled with rage and anger. It took a moment for the significance of McCann's words to sink in.

He looked McCann in the eyes, and in that moment he knew exactly what the man meant. If he was honest with himself, he'd known all along. He'd been arrogant. He'd been desperate. He'd been stupid. And he knew what came next, if it hadn't already happened.

Before he knew what he was doing, Jack was running through McCann's hallway, back down the steps and towards his car.

45

After a few minutes, he realised he was driving aimlessly. He pulled his car over to the side of the road, switched off the engine and just sat.

He didn't know what to do. Through the fog of anger, resentment and betrayal, there was one thing Jack couldn't ignore. McCann's threat had been clear: Frank's life was in danger. But it wasn't as if Jack could just drop him a quick text in prison to let him know. In any case, what good would it do?

Whatever happened, he needed Frank alive. McCann was right: he'd been bullshitting about a couple of his goons going rogue, and Frank was Jack's best hope — his only hope — of ever nailing anything on McCann.

His first instinct was to call the prison. He was pretty sure he'd be able to get through to the governor. But he had no way of knowing how far McCann's tentacles stretched. He'd already been blindsided — many times — by the people he'd had on his side over the years, and it wouldn't have surprised Jack in the slightest to find out McCann had the governor of the prison onside, too.

There was only one person with any greater authority whom Jack felt — hoped — he could trust. He pulled out his phone and called Chief Constable Charles Hawes, hoping he'd answer his phone. After four rings, the call connected.

'Jack, can I call you back in a bit? I'm about to go into a meeting.'

'No, sir. Sorry. It's urgent.'

There was a moment of silence as Hawes registered the tension in Jack's voice. 'What is it?' he asked.

'It's Frank Vine. He's in danger. We've just received a credible threat from Gary McCann.'

'What sort of threat?'

Jack struggled to remember the words. 'I dunno. He said Frank wasn't safe. He said... Sir, I was looking him in the eyes when he said it. He means it. Frank's the only chance we've got of nailing McCann. We can't risk anything happening to him.'

'Well you've changed your tune.'

'I know. And I... Look, you just have to trust me, sir. I can't tell you why. Not now. But I met with Frank recently. I visited him. He wants to testify. He's changed his mind. He wants to help us send McCann down. We need him alive.'

'I'll call the prison. I'll let them know there's been a threat. We'll get them to keep an eye on him.'

Jack sighed. 'Can we trust them? He's already been attacked at least once. We don't know how far McCann's influence reaches. I'm almost certain he'll have people on the inside.'

'What else can we do, Jack?' Hawes said. 'We can't send our own armed guards in there. The prison system is secure. That's kind of the whole point of it.'

'Is it, though? Nothing's ever secure, is it?'

As Jack had moved on through life, it had become more and more apparent to him that absolutely any position could be corrupted. Money would always talk, and those on the wrong side of the law would always have more money than those on the correct side. It wasn't outside the realms of reason to think a prison governor could be corrupted by money or outside influence. He'd seen it in the police. He was sure he'd seen it in the courts. The whole world had seen it in politics. So what of a fairly indistinct regional British prison?

'Jack, it's all we've got,' Hawes said. 'We can get a message to the governor, or to Frank himself, but if you suspect the management's involved, what's either of them going to be able — or willing — to do about it?'

'I know, but—'

'Do you want me to call them or not?'

Jack thought for a moment. He didn't see he had much choice. 'Alright. Yeah,' he said. 'Call them.'

46

Jack and Wendy sat down opposite Clive Blake in the interview room. Something didn't quite sit right with Wendy. Clive looked so out of place, this relatively meek and mild-mannered man, a parent, arrested on suspicion of having paid Connor French to murder his daughter's boyfriend.

He certainly didn't seem like the sort of man who'd effectively hire a hitman, but Wendy had to admit she'd seen it all over the years. The idea that one could spot a criminal on sight was laughable.

She often thought back to one of her first shifts as a uniformed police constable, when she'd been out in a patrol car with a colleague, looking for a man who they suspected of beating a teenage boy to within an inch of his life, all for a Nokia mobile phone and twenty quid in cash. The only description they had to go on was that their suspect was wearing a red top. A few minutes later they'd spotted a twenty-something male swaggering down a dark road, shaved head and stubble, with a cigarette in his mouth. And, of course, a red top. His excuse of having 'just gone out for a walk' hadn't washed with either of them, and he'd been arrested on the spot on suspicion of assault and robbery. By the time they'd got him into an interview suite, it turned out he was the first violinist with a major symphony orchestra, and had indeed 'just gone out for a walk'. Their suspect appeared at the reception desk the next morning, a weedy, geeky looking kid who'd been dragged in by his mother after coming down for breakfast the next morning with a bloodied fist and a new Nokia.

And now, as Clive Blake sat opposite her, inextricably linked by solid evidence to the death of Matthew Hulford, even his solicitor looked more like a criminal mastermind than he did.

Jack started the interview and got the formalities out of the way, before leading with his first question. She could tell something wasn't quite right with him, but that was nothing new for Jack Culverhouse. He quite often turned up at work looking like a bulldog chewing a wasp.

'First of all,' he said, 'can you tell me the nature of your relationship with Matthew Hulford?'

'Yes, he was my daughter's boyfriend.'

'Your daughter being Jennifer Blake?'

'Jenny, yes.'

'And did you get on with him?'

'He seemed like a nice enough lad. Quiet.'

'Were you aware of his... extra-curricular activities?'

'You mean the drugs?'

'Yes, the drugs.'

'No.'

'You didn't know he was dealing drugs?'

'No.'

'Okay. What do you do for a living, Clive?'

'I'm a senior analyst for a data storage firm.'

'Sounds exciting.'

'It has its moments.'

'Pay well?'

'Pretty well.'

'Life must be pretty comfortable, then? Nice little nest egg in the savings account?'

Clive cocked his head slightly. 'Not when you've got two kids and a wife who likes to spend money, no.'

'You had a fair amount in your savings accounts up until recently, though, didn't you?'

Jack looked at Clive and left that question hanging. He wanted to make it clear they'd been able to gather quite a lot of information about his financial affairs in a relatively short space of time, without actually giving anything away just yet.

'I'm not sure what you mean,' Clive replied.

'I mean you had quite a fair amount in savings up until recently. In fact, over the past couple of months, you withdrew more than twenty-thousand pounds in twelve separate cash withdrawals. That's a lot of money to pull out of your savings. New kitchen, was it?'

'Various things. It's been an expensive year and quiet on the work front. These things fluctuate. It happens.'

'Lots of bills?'

'Some of it, yes.'

'And they all needed paying in cash, did they?'

Clive's solicitor leaned forward. 'It isn't an offence to withdraw money from your savings accounts as and when you wish. My client's perfectly entitled to do so.'

'Absolutely. But if there's suspicion that cash might have either been obtained illegally or used for nefarious purposes, then we have every right not only to investigate, but to ask questions. And if your client has nothing to hide, he should be perfectly comfortable answering them. So. Clive. Twenty grand in two months is a lot of expenditure, even if your missus does like her handbags. Who is she, Tallulah Bankhead?'

'With the greatest of respect,' the solicitor said, 'unless you have any material evidence that my client's money has been used for illegal purposes, I'd strongly recommend this line of questioning continues no further.'

'Okay. Let's try something a little different,' Jack said, placing a photograph in front of them. 'Do you recognise the item in the photograph, Clive?'

'It looks like a carrier bag.'

'It is.' Jack put another photo on top of it. 'This is what we found when we opened the carrier bag. Do you recognise it?'

'It looks like cash.'

'Correct. Twenty-five thousand pounds, in fact. Do you know where we found this?'

'No.'

'It was in a storage locker in town. Nothing else in

there. Just this. Lot of money. Do you know who the storage locker was registered to?'

'No,' Clive said softly.

'It's registered to Connor French. Do you recognise that name?'

Clive didn't say anything.

'He's Matthew Hulford's best friend. Was. Do you know him?'

'You don't need to answer their questions, Clive,' the solicitor said. 'You can respond with "no comment" if you'd prefer.'

'Okay, Clive,' Jack said. 'See, I've got a bit of a problem here. I've met Connor French. A few times, in fact. We've had him in custody. But then you probably already knew that. I imagine word's got around. Now, I don't know about you, but to me it seems like twenty-five grand is a lot of money for a kid of his age. Especially in cash. Don't you think?'

'If you say so.'

'The thing is, a lot of that cash was withdrawn from banks as fresh notes. I'm not sure if you've ever noticed, but banknotes have serial numbers on them. That means it's possible to trace where it was issued, which accounts it's passed through and where it's gone. Each time it comes back through a bank, it's logged. Now, these banknotes here made our jobs a lot easier, because a lot of them were numbered sequentially. Twelve different sequences, in fact. And the banks were able to tell us when those notes were withdrawn, and who withdrew them. Do you want to say anything?'

'No comment.'

'The banknotes were withdrawn by you, weren't they Clive?'

'No comment.'

'Clive, the banks have confirmed it was you who withdrew the banknotes. They were withdrawn from your accounts. Does anyone else have access to your accounts?'

'No comment.'

'Clive, did you pay Connor French twenty-five thousand pounds so he would murder Matthew Hulford and keep him away from your daughter?'

The solicitor leaned forward again. 'I think we'll pause proceedings there, thank you. I'd like some time to speak with my client.'

47

If anyone had asked Terry Carter as a child what job he'd be doing at this age, prison officer wouldn't've even been in his first twenty guesses. Hell, if someone asked him five years ago the result would've been the same. But redundancy from the theatre meant he'd been desperate for work — any work — and he'd been amazed to discover just how accessible this job had been. Then again, how many people fancied spending their days in prison, even if they were getting paid for it?

But when all was said and done, Terry didn't mind the job. At the end of the day, it was work, and it'd come at a time when he would've been grateful for just about any job. He'd always been under the impression that prison officers had to be big, beefy blokes who'd otherwise be working as bouncers or trainers in gyms, but it turns out that couldn't have been further from the truth. He'd mentioned it at his interview, and been told that having a bunch of bruisers walking around the prison tended to attract more trouble than anything, as they became walking targets for prisoners who were keen to claim the most impressive scalp possible to increase their social standing inside.

Did he see himself working here until he retired? If he was honest, he hoped not. He wasn't sure he could hack it in his sixties. But then again, could he have seen himself setting up lighting rigs at the same age? At least he'd developed a passion for that.

For Terry, evening lock-up signified — quite naturally — the end of the day. From that point on, all would be — or at least should be — quiet. With the prisoners back in their cells, and assuming none of them decided to start a riot or murder each other, it should be a case of simply seeing out the rest of his shift, before heading home to bed. Sandra would probably be asleep by then — she usually was when he was on this shift — but, after twenty-five years of marriage, that hardly concerned him.

Now, all that was left to do was to take a quick peek into each cell, just to make sure it did indeed have the correct number of prisoners and that no-one was tunnelling out through the walls Shawshank-style, and then he'd be able to put his feet up.

He wandered down the corridor to the next cell, pulled open the flap and looked in. The prisoner didn't jump, didn't pay him any attention and didn't respond. It was all part of the daily routine. He carried on down the corridor, carried on checking cells, until he got to the end of the row.

He pulled open the last flap and peered inside. No. *No no.*

He called for backup on his radio, then unlocked the door and went inside.

The prisoner was sitting on the cold floor, slumped with his back against the cold wall, blood pooling around him.

'Shit,' John, his colleague, cursed as he came into the cell behind him. 'Is he alive?'

'I dunno. I don't think so. Look at him.'

'How the fuck's he done that, the silly bastard? Who the fuck gave him razor blades?'

'I don't know. Jesus. Fucking hell, what a mess. He's done his wrists. Fucking hell, it's hit the ceiling! Is that normal?'

'If you get it right, it is. Frank? Frank, can you hear me? There's no pulse. When was he last checked on?'

'Lock-up. I didn't do the check, but there was nothing reported. How quickly do you bleed out from something like that?'

'Pretty fucking quickly. He's gone down the length of the artery, look. That's the way to do it. Some silly bastards go across the wrist, but then it just clots and heals itself. He's done it properly, at least.'

Even at moments like this, dark humour tended to prevail in this job. It wasn't the first time they'd found someone in this state, and it certainly wouldn't be the last.

Terry pulled the bedsheets off Frank's bed and tried to tie them round the wounds on his wrists, but it all seemed futile. The blood, which had initially come out with enough force to hit the ceiling and walls, was now barely dribbling from his wrists.

'Terry, mate, there's no point. Look at him. He's grey. There's no pulse. He's gone.'

48

Jack closed the Chief Constable's office door behind him, and stood for a moment in the corridor.

He knew it'd take him some time to process his emotions, which seemed to either come to him all at once or not at all. There were moments when he was deluged by anger, sadness, regret, fear, fury and the overwhelming urge to self-implode, but that was all interspersed with periods where he felt absolutely nothing.

Charles Hawes's call had gone in to the governor a little earlier, but it had already been too late. Again, Jack felt overwhelmed with anger and fury towards Gary McCann.

Their relationship had always been complex, but he'd believed McCann to be a man of his word. There'd been a grudging respect for years. Now he realised the man was nothing but a cunt who'd sell his own grandmother if it gained him an advantage. And that was before his thoughts even turned to Frank.

Frank had been his friend and colleague for years, but his betrayal had destroyed almost everything they'd had. It had certainly destroyed the respect Jack had for him. If Jack had been asked a few days earlier whether he cared what happened to Frank, he would've said no. As far as he was concerned, Frank was merely his route to nailing Gary McCann. He'd lost all other status in Jack's mind. But Jack had been surprised by how hard the news of Frank's death had hit him.

More than anything else, it all seemed such a ridiculous waste. A long career, a decent life, all thrown away in pursuit of cash and ending in a pool of blood on the floor of a prison cell. What was the point? What had the previous years been for? And now there was absolutely no chance whatsoever of redemption. The one thing Frank had which could have potentially salvaged some aspect of his reputation was his ability to testify against McCann and help bring him down. Now he didn't even have that, and nor did Jack.

His thoughts turned to how his family would hear the news. It would be usual for the Chief Constable to inform the family of the death of a police officer, but did Frank deserve that honour? Would it be left to Jack as his former colleague and friend? In a way, Jack felt it was his duty. It was certainly preferable to a faceless PC going round and delivering the news. He was quite sure Frank's family wouldn't want that. Nor would Frank.

But did it matter what Frank wanted? Frank had always done whatever he wanted, and look where that'd got him. He'd hardly earned the right to call the shots —

not if you made the assumption that his years of service had been completely wiped out by his recent corruption. That 'if' was one Jack bounced around in his mind over and over again.

He didn't know how long he'd been standing outside that door, but he quickly realised his thoughts weren't going to clear any time soon, and he wandered back down the corridor in the direction of his office. He was barely a few yards away when the door to the incident room opened and Debbie Weston came bursting out.

'Ah. There you are, guv. We've just had a call from the search teams on the scene at Clive Blake's house. They've found something buried in the garden. A bag of blood-stained clothes.'

'Okay. That's good. That's good, Debbie.'

'Are you alright? You look a bit pale.'

'Uh. Yeah. Fine. I, uh…'

Jack looked at Debbie, one of his most loyal and unassuming colleagues. Even through all the issues in her personal life, she'd been steadfast in her determination. She'd never sought or encouraged promotion, happy to remain a Detective Constable, yet more often than not being the one who uncovered that crucial piece of information which unlocked the case. He silently admonished himself for allowing Frank's actions to destroy his trust of absolutely anybody, and steeled himself to deliver the news.

'I just got back from the Chief Constable's office, Debbie. He had some bad news. Frank died earlier this evening.'

'Oh.' Debbie took a few moments to absorb the news. 'What happened?' she asked.

'You don't want to know. Let's just leave it at that for now. So. Clive Blake. Uh, are they running tests on the blood?'

'Yeah. Will be a couple of days before we get results. But it's got to be Matthew's blood. It implicates Clive more heavily if he's been hiding the clothes. Explains how Connor got away with it for so long, too.' Debbie sighed. 'Look, is this the time for us to be doing this? We can leave it until the news has sunk in. We can get an extension.'

Jack shook his head. 'No. No, I need a distraction.'

49

Jack had made the deliberate decision not to tell Wendy what'd happened to Frank until after they'd interviewed Clive Blake again, at the very earliest. He wanted her to have a clear mind and to drive the interview. He was in no fit state to do so, after all. He'd asked Debbie not to mention anything to anyone else. The others had all gone home for the night anyway, and he felt it would be more fitting to address everyone at the morning briefing.

As he sat behind the table in the interview room, opposite Clive Blake and his solicitor, Jack wondered what Gary McCann was doing at that moment. He could picture him sitting in his living room, drinking champagne with Helen, arms round each other as McCann beamed from ear to ear at how fucking clever he was. Not only had he escaped justice yet again, but he'd managed to get another one over on Jack by moving his own fucking wife into the house. The man's smugness and ego knew no bounds. All Jack wanted to do was get out of this interview room, drive over to McCann's house and kick his fucking head in. And he knew that was exactly what McCann wanted. Whatever Jack did, he was one step ahead.

'Clive, we're interviewing you again this evening because some new evidence has come to light,' Wendy said, calm and professional, oblivious to everything that'd happened. 'I don't know if you're aware, but we've had search teams at your property since your arrest. They're trained to look for evidence and items which might be of interest to our investigation. Do you understand that?'

'Yes, of course I do. And if you've been trashing my house and taking furniture apart, I damn well hope it'll be absolutely pristine by the time you've left, or I'll be dragging you through the courts to pay for every last penny. It's a huge invasion of privacy, that's what it is.'

'Why are you so angry, Clive?' Jack asked, noticing the change in the man's attitude.

Clive threw his arms up in the air and made a noise like a van stopping on gravel. 'Oh, come on. You've locked me up in here, throwing all sorts of accusations around, and now you tell me you're harassing my family and taking my house apart. What do you want me to do, breakdance?'

'No, we expect you to cooperate so this can all be over and done with as quickly as possible,' Wendy said. 'It's in everybody's best interests. Now, during their search of your property, the team discovered something of interest buried in your back garden. Do you have any idea what that might be?'

'No. But I'm sure you're about to tell me.'

Wendy passed over a photo of a muddied carrier bag, opened just enough to see some fabric inside. 'Do you recognise this?'

'No.'

'It's a Sainsbury's carrier bag with some clothing inside. Ring any bells?'

'No.'

'That was found buried in your garden, Clive. Any idea how it might have got there?'

'No.'

'Do you have a gardener, perhaps?'

'No.'

'Clive, I have to tell you there's heavy blood staining on that clothing. It's currently undergoing tests to identify whose blood it is. Do you want to say anything to that?'

'No.'

'Did you agree to hide the bloodstained clothing for Connor French so he wouldn't get caught?'

'No.'

Jack tensed his jaw and bit his tongue, but it was no use. 'Oh, for crying out loud! Everyone can see it, Clive. I can see it. DS Knight can see it. That gormless tit sitting next to you can see it. And I sure as hell know you can see it. You handed twenty-five grand in cash over to Connor French, who was seen walking Matthew Hulford to Mildenheath Woods on the night he died, then returning alone. We found the knife with Matthew's blood and Connor's fingerprints on it. Did you try disposing of that, too? You chose to hide the clothes in your garden. Were you going to chuck those in the bin next week? Spread it out a bit, maybe? Try to keep the evidence away from Connor French?'

'No.'

'Let me tell you something, Clive,' Jack said, his voice a deep growl. 'I am fucking *sick* of people lying to me. I've had *enough* of people trying to deceive me. The evidence is all here that you paid Connor French to kill Matthew, then tried covering up for him. Now the least you can do is be a fucking man about it and have the decency to admit to everyone what you've done.'

Wendy leaned forward, towards the recording machine. 'Okay, we're pausing the interview there for a moment. Sir, can I have a quick chat outside, please?'

Jack and Wendy left the room, and Jack paced the corridor outside, trying to massage the stress from his temples.

'What the hell was that all about?' Wendy asked.

'Don't speak to superior officers like that, Knight. I don't need your bullshit as well.'

'As well as what? What's going on?'

Jack sighed. 'Frank's dead.'

'What? How? When?'

'Earlier tonight. He was found in a pool of blood in his cell. Slashed his wrists.'

'Shit. Why the hell would he do that?'

'I didn't say he did.'

'What, you think someone killed him? Who? Why?'

'Can I fill you in on this a little later, perhaps? I've got more than enough to get my head around right now without having to go into all the details. Let's just say things are about to kick off big time.'

'Jesus. When did you find out?'

'An hour ago, maybe a bit more. I went to see him recently. He wanted to testify against McCann. He said he had intel that could help bring him down. I looked into his eyes and I believed him. He was telling the truth. For fucking once.'

'And you think McCann had him killed to stop him telling all?'

'I can't tell you what I think right now. I don't even know myself. Fucking hell, it never rains but it pours.'

'Look, we can take a few minutes to get our heads straight, then restart the interview later, alright?'

'Whatever. Let's just get it done. I don't want that bastard wriggling on the hook any longer. Let's at least get one bit of good news out of today.'

The door to the interview room opened and Clive Blake's solicitor stepped into the corridor, a sour look on his face.

'You can fuck off as well,' Jack said, not even looking at him. 'I know I lost my rag, but you'll have to deal with it.'

'Detective Chief Inspector, if I could just—'

'No, you can't. We'll restart the interview in a few

minutes. And your client had better bloody well be willing to answer some questions.'

'That's what I came out to tell you,' the solicitor said, looking utterly beaten. 'Mr Blake just told me he's ready to talk. In his words, he says he "can't handle it anymore". He wants to tell you everything.'

50

Clive Blake had a very different air about him when they stepped back into the interview room. The calm defiance had gone, replaced by a sense that this was a man who'd finally realised it was over. It was a transformation they'd seen many times before, but it never failed to have an impact.

'You can do this in a pre-prepared written statement if you prefer,' Wendy said. 'We'll need a statement anyway.'

Clive shook his head. 'No. Not yet. I want to talk first. Writing it down is too... cold. I want to be able to explain everything properly. I want you to see I'm sincere.'

'Okay. We're listening.'

Clive swallowed and began to speak. 'I'm not some sort of career criminal, okay? I'm guessing you already know that. All I am is a man desperate to protect his daughter. She's got everything going for her, and all I've ever wanted is the best for her. I could see her throwing her life away, but there was no way of telling her that. She wasn't listening. She's so bright, so clever, so intelligent. She could have anything she wanted. She can go as far as she likes. But she was spending all her time hanging around with this... this criminal. What else can you call him? A drug dealer. I saw the impact it had on her. I watched her confidence disappear. Her pride. Her hopes and dreams. I tried speaking to her about it, of course I did. But she wasn't having any of it. She kept saying he was going to change, but the only thing changing was her. It was getting worse.

'I knew something had to be done. It was either him or her. There was no other way out. I can't say it often enough — all I ever wanted was to protect my daughter. You need to believe me. I spent weeks agonising over it. Months, even. I didn't know what to do. I thought about hiring a hitman, but I don't know anything about that. I mean, where the hell do you start with something like that? You can't just look them up on Google, can you? I knew it was going to cost money, though, so I started taking some out of the savings accounts and putting it to one side. I didn't want to trip any alarms by drawing it all out at once, and I was pretty sure whoever did it wasn't going to take payment by BACS.

'Then an idea came to me. Matthew knew bad people, people who were more than happy to trade their consciences for money. And the more I thought about that, the more it made sense. I found Connor. I discovered through Jenny that he was Matthew's best friend, and that he was involved in all this shady business. The thought came to me that I should approach Connor and persuade him to get rid of Matthew. By that point I had nearly twenty grand together in cash. I thought that'd be more than enough for a kid of his age. I mean, it's a house deposit, isn't it? I thought, that'll be enough to get him out of the drugs game too. If it's all about money, he'll be able to set himself up for life, get a proper job and it'll have the added benefit that Matthew would be out of Jenny's life, too. It was the perfect plan.'

Clive seemed to stop talking for a few moments, hanging his head with his chin against his chest as he processed his shame and tried to work out what to say next.

'You can take all the time you want,' Wendy said. 'You're doing really well and being very honest. We appreciate that. It'll give everyone a lot of closure, too.'

Clive shook his head. 'No. No, you don't get it. That's not what happened at all. Not in the end. I just…'

'It's okay, Clive,' Wendy said. 'I can tell it's a big thing for you. Would it help if we ran through what we know, and you can clarify things or let us know if we've got anything wrong?'

Clive shrugged.

'Okay,' Wendy continued. 'So let's stick on the subject of the money for now. You mentioned twenty thousand pounds. We found twenty-five thousand in a storage unit registered to Connor French. Did all that money come from you, or was it just the twenty thousand?'

'No, it was all from me.'

'Okay. And did you give him that money before or

after he killed Matthew? Was it half upfront, something like that?'

Clive shook his head. 'No. No, that's not how it happened.'

'It's okay. Take your time. We just want to get to the bottom of things. The details help, believe me. It helps put things into context for loved ones, and it can even make things simpler when it comes to court. It makes it more human. That can help.'

'It's not about detail. We're not onto detail yet. We're nowhere near. You've got it all wrong.'

'What do you mean?' Wendy asked, cocking her head.

'You've got it all wrong. I didn't give Connor the money so he'd kill Matthew. I gave him the money to keep quiet. So he wouldn't tell anyone.'

'Tell anyone what, Clive?'

'That I killed Matthew.'

51

It was as if a lightbulb had switched on in Wendy's head. It all made sense now. Connor luring Matthew to the woods, coming out with clean clothes apart from a bit of mud on his trainers. He hadn't had to do a thing. Not really. Just get Matthew there, keep quiet, and net twenty-five grand.

But there were questions left unanswered. Why were Connor's prints on the knife? How did it end up in the wheelie bin? Why did Connor agree to keep Clive's secret?

'What happened, Clive?' Wendy asked.

'I knew I had to do something. But the more I thought about it, the more I knew it had to be me who did it. The more people who were involved, the more likely it was someone would spill the beans. I had to keep it to myself. I couldn't have anyone else involved. I got Matthew's number from Jenny's phone. I bought a pay-as-you-go mobile. A burner, they call it. Topped it up with cash. And I contacted him. Told him I'd got his number from a friend and that I wanted to buy cannabis. We arranged to meet in the woods. At that point, I knew what I was going to do. I drove up there just as it was getting dark, and took a shovel, some tape, a change of clothes and a few other bits into the woods and put them somewhere I didn't think they'd be found over the next few hours. Then it got towards ten o'clock. Jenny was working late, and my wife had already gone to bed. I told myself that if she woke up, couldn't find me and rang me, I'd say I'd gone out for a walk or something. I didn't have much time to think about it. It all happened so quickly. I had to just go for it.

'I got dressed into a few scruffy old clothes I kept for decorating, put on a hat and some gloves and went over to the woods. I'd arranged to meet Matthew right next to where I'd hidden the shovel. I'd planned to catch him off guard, and hit him round the head with it as soon as he arrived. I didn't want a conversation. I wanted it over with. But then I saw two of them. So I pulled my hat down a bit and hunched my shoulders and tried to deepen my voice, but I don't think it was that convincing. We were talking for a minute or two, but I could tell they both knew something was up. I made eye contact with Connor at one point and I could see he recognised me. I think Matthew did, too, because he told Connor he should go back home.

'They spoke to each other, but I couldn't hear what they were saying. I thought I saw Connor handing something to Matthew, but at the time I wasn't sure. When Connor was gone, Matthew tried calling me out. He told me to stop bullshitting him and to tell him why I'd really asked him to come out here. He wasn't afraid of me in the slightest. I don't know for certain that he knew who I was. I think he did, but I knew I either had to run or just do it. Right there, right then. If I ran, that'd be it. Jenny's future would be ruined and he'd be constantly on his guard. I only had one chance. I even thought for a moment he might run after me and kill me instead. I didn't know what to think. But then he just shook his head and turned around. He was going to walk away. He thought I was that sad and pathetic, I wasn't even worth talking to. I knew in that moment he didn't have a care in the world for anyone but himself. So I went for him. I started punching him, hitting him. I just went berserk. I put my arm around his neck and I squeezed and squeezed until he dropped to his knees. He was gasping for breath, but I managed to get his hands behind his back and tie them tightly. Then I taped his mouth so he wouldn't scream or yell. I turned to go and get the shovel before I changed my mind, and that's when I saw the flick knife, half hanging out of his jacket pocket. I realised that was what Connor must have given him when I saw something handed over. By this point, I'd tied Matthew up, and I was pretty certain they both knew who I was. I know what sort of circles they're involved in. There was only one way out. It made sense straight away. I took the flick knife out of his pocket, opened it up, then slit his throat.

'I made sure I was standing behind him when I did it,

so I didn't get too much blood over me. I was amazed at how quickly he bled out. His head just sort of dropped forward and he fell onto his side. I started digging, but it took forever. The ground was hard and there were tree roots everywhere. I don't think anyone knows how hard it is to dig a grave, especially somewhere like that. I'd dragged his body a bit further away from the main path, but I couldn't quite manage to get it as far as I wanted. I dug as far as I could, but I couldn't go any further. I laid him in as flat as I could, and covered him with earth, then tried shovelling leaves and all sorts of other stuff on top. I thought it'd be okay for a bit, but there was no doubt he was going to be found. I stood there for a while and made sure I'd covered all my tracks. I'd been wearing gloves the whole time. The knife wasn't mine. I couldn't see there'd be any forensic traces, and in any case I didn't see how I'd be a suspect. It's not as if I could just take it all back anyway, is it? So I changed into my other clothes, got everything together and went home.

'I was awake all night, panicking, worrying about what was going to happen next. When I knew Connor hadn't told anyone he'd seen me, the penny dropped. He'd realised Matthew had his knife, and figured out that's what'd been used to kill him. He must've known I had the knife, and that his prints would be all over it, so he didn't want to send the police my way. A few days later, I stopped him in the street and handed over a carrier bag full of notes. I told him I wouldn't talk if he didn't, then I walked off home. He had the cash, I had the knife, and we both had our secrets. When Connor was arrested, I panicked. Big time. But as the hours and days went on, I realised he still hadn't told anyone it was me. I knew I had to get rid of the evidence, just in case. The night before the bins were collected, I went for a walk and put the knife in a random wheelie bin. The clothes were buried in the garden, so I thought I had a bit more time with those. I told myself that if I got away with the knife, I'd do the clothes the fortnight after, or have a bonfire in the garden and get rid of them that way. I don't know what else to say.'

Wendy let out a breath she'd been holding for some time. 'Well, that's quite a lot to take in, Clive.'

'It's a lot to get out. Trust me. I know what I did was wrong. I know I'm going to spend a lot of time in prison. But I don't regret what I did. I'd spend a hundred years inside if it stops Jenny from being imprisoned in that life. She's got a chance now. She can do everything she wants to do. She can be the best she can be. What other choice did I have? I was only trying to protect her.'

Jack looked at the man in front of him, the man who'd just admitted the pre-meditated murder of a young lad, and felt an unusual and unexpected sympathy.

Before he could speak, or even think of the words to say, he was distracted by his phone ringing in his pocket. Chrissie was calling him. He pressed to reject the call, and went back to the interview. Barely a moment later, the phone rang again. 'Sorry, I'm going to have to take this,' he said.

He stepped out of the interview room and answered the call. 'Chrissie, I'm in the middle of an interview at the moment, can I call you back in a bit?'

'No, Jack. Something's happened. We need you. Emily's been rushed into hospital.'

52

Jack parked his car in a side road near the hospital without even bothering to check for parking restrictions. Fines and penalties were an irrelevance right now. He desperately needed to see Emily, needed to make sure she was okay.

Chrissie hadn't given him much information on the phone — only that Emily had shown signs of early labour but had also begun to bleed. He didn't need the details at that point — he'd just needed to get there, to be with her, to be there for her.

He jogged up the road towards the maternity unit of Mildenheath Hospital, panting Emily's name at the receptionist as he got there, trying to recapture his breath enough to explain the circumstances and find out what was going on. The receptionist called for a doctor or midwife to come down, and Jack had an arduous wait of barely a couple of minutes, but which felt like hours.

He paced the reception area, desperate to kick the

doors down and find Emily for himself, but he knew he needed to keep a level head. Emily would likely be distressed, anxious and worked up herself, and it wouldn't do anybody any good if he joined them in the same state. If things had gone wrong, she was going to need him more than ever, and he needed to remain calm and strong for her.

Just as he was managing to steel his nerves, the door opened and a doctor appeared, introducing herself as Claire Evans.

'Mr Culverhouse, would you like to come with me?' Dr Evans said, her tone professional and giving nothing away.

'How is she?' Jack asked. 'Is the baby okay?'

'Both are stable at the moment, but I must stress that in these sorts of situations, things can change very quickly indeed.'

'What situation? What's actually happened? I don't know anything.'

'It appears that Emily's gone into very early labour. Dangerously early, in fact. There's also been some bleeding, which we're trying to find the source of via scans as we speak. The good news is the baby has a good heart rate, but we've administered Emily a drug called terbutaline. It's a tocolytic; it'll help to prevent and slow the contractions of the uterus and will delay labour.'

'For how long?'

'It's difficult to say. At most, probably forty-eight hours.'

'Jesus Christ. She can't give birth within forty-eight

hours. She's nowhere near ready. The baby's nowhere near ready.'

'Indeed,' Dr Evans said, her face serious. 'That's precisely why it's such a serious situation. But she's in the best possible hands. First we need to find the source of the bleeding. Once we've done that, we can determine the problem and, hopefully, solve it.'

'What about a c-section or something? What happens if you need to get the baby out?'

'That's a distinct possibility. If Emily's having problems which might put the baby's life — or hers — at risk, we'll have to come to a decision about that. But that certainly doesn't minimise risks. If anything, it carries risks all of its own. The chances of a foetus that young surviving outside of the mother are very slim.'

Jack felt his heart lurch in his chest. 'And what about the chances of it surviving inside?'

'It's difficult to say right now. I hope you can appreciate that. All I can say is if the baby was happy and thriving, labour wouldn't be happening at this extremely early stage. I'll be completely honest with you. We're doing everything we can, but I really don't want to get your hopes up unnecessarily. Whichever way you look at it, it's an extremely serious situation.'

Jack felt a huge swell of emotion rising inside him. 'Can I see her?' he croaked.

Dr Evans smiled and nodded. 'Follow me.'

53

There was never any doubt in Clive's mind as to who should be the recipient of his allowed phone call. There was a good chance he wouldn't be able to see either of them for a while, but the very least he wanted was to ensure they understood why.

He listened as the phone rang, and continued to ring. Just as he thought no-one might answer, the call connected.

'Hello?' came the familiar voice.

'Aretha. It's me. Listen, I don't know how much time they're going to give me. Is Jenny there?'

His wife stayed silent for a moment or two before speaking, her voice soft. 'Yes. She's here.'

'Can I—'

'She doesn't want to speak to you.'

Those words pierced through Clive like a crossbow bolt. 'Oh. Okay. Look, I need her to know why I did what

I did. She might not be ready to hear it yet, but it's important she knows.'

'Important to who?'

'To everyone.'

'What, and you think it's going to make the blindest bit of difference? Do you really think it's going to change anything?'

Clive tensed his jaw. 'Probably not. But I need to—'

'If you're only doing it for yourself, then don't bother.'

'I'm not. I... How is everyone?'

'How do you think?'

'I'm sorry, Aretha.'

'You're *sorry*? Do you think that makes it all better? Clive, I've spent the last couple of weeks sleeping next to a killer! Did any of that ever cross your mind? The damage it would do to everybody else, just because you felt like you wanted to play bloody Superdad?'

'It wasn't like that... I did it for Jenny. To protect her.'

'Oh, listen to yourself, Clive! She's a grown woman. She doesn't need anybody telling her what she can and can't do, and she definitely doesn't need what happened to... Oh for Christ's sake, Clive. What the bloody hell have you done?'

Clive swallowed as he listened to his wife sob. 'I can't change it now, Aretha. What's happened has happened. I'm going to deal with the fallout as best I can, but I imagine that'll take quite some time.'

Aretha's voice was almost a whisper. 'You never could get out of your own head, could you? You genuinely have no idea of the effect this has had on anyone else, do you?'

'Of course I do. I—'

'You don't, Clive,' Aretha said, stopping him dead in his tracks. 'If you did, you wouldn't be calling here. We have nothing to say to you, and nothing we want to hear from you. You think you saved Jenny? You haven't saved anything. You've *destroyed* her. She'll spend the rest of her life knowing her father was a murderer, a murderer who killed her own boyfriend in cold blood. Who took him out into the woods, tied him up and slit his bloody—'

'Mum!' came Jenny's voice in the background.

'Can I speak to her? Please.'

'No, Clive. You've ruined everything. The only person who can protect Jenny now is me, and I'm protecting her by making sure murderers don't get in contact with her. I suggest you don't call here again. We don't want to hear it. We'll be at your trial to watch you get sentenced. Until then, goodbye, Clive.'

54

Jack watched as the curtains slowly drew across in front of the coffin. It was, in more ways than once, closure. But how could closure ever really be achieved after all that had happened?

He wiped a tear from the corner of his eye. It was all such a waste. Such an extraordinary waste.

The turnout had been good. It was, in many ways, heartwarming to see how many friends and colleagues had turned out to pay their respects and say goodbye. The news had, of course, come as a shock to Jack, but he'd at least had a small amount of time to prepare for it, and it hadn't been entirely unexpected.

In many ways, it would be the beginning of a new era, the start of a new chapter. But whichever idiom or cliché Jack put on it, nothing could persuade him that it had all been so completely unnecessary.

They'd all got their hopes up. He certainly had. It was looking very much like the future would be filled with beaming smiles and a sense that all was right with the world, but that now couldn't happen. At least, not for some time.

Jack looked around at the other mourners. Everyone from the young to the old seemed to be here, and he realised yet again that the one thing that managed to unite everyone was death. It was also the great divider, of course. Everyone knew families who'd been torn apart by tragedy, or even just the banal ridiculousness of squabbling over a will or inheritance, as if it was ever right to argue over another person's money or wishes.

There would be no disagreement over inheritance or wills here, though. In many ways, this would be much more straightforward, even though it was no less heartbreaking and upsetting for everyone involved.

Outside the crematorium, Wendy sidled over to him. 'How you doing?' she asked.

'Oh yeah. Brilliant. Might come up here every day if I've got nothing else on. You?'

Wendy shrugged. 'What can I say? What can anyone say? It was a good service.'

Jack let out a snort. 'Why do people say that? Of course it wasn't a good bloody service. It was a funeral. We're only here because someone's died, so we thought we'd chuck them in a box and set fire to them. Absolutely fucking bizarre, when you think about it. And who's rating these things, anyway?'

'There'll be a website somewhere, I bet you. Anyway, that's the worst bit out of the way. People only come to funerals for the fun bit afterwards. Speaking of which, do you want a lift back from the Albert later? We can run your car home now, if you like. Save you picking it up in the morning.'

Jack thought about this for a moment. 'Nah,' he said, eventually. 'I'm not really in the mood for drinking, to be honest with you. Or partying, celebrating, whatever you want to call it.'

'Remembering?'

'Yeah. That can get fucked, 'n all. Remembering's the last thing I want to be doing right now.'

'Okay,' Wendy said. 'Well, if you're happier looking into the future, there was something I want to let you know.'

Jack looked at her. 'Don't tell me you're fucking pregnant, for Christ's sake. We're stretched enough as it is. If we lose another body we'll all be up in Milton House before we can say "Up yours, Malcolm Pope".'

Wendy laughed. 'No. Don't worry. I'm not pregnant. In fact, it'll probably make things a lot easier for you. I've finally put in for my inspector's exams.'

'Bloody hell. That took you long enough. When's the next one?'

'Few months, so you don't have to worry about me nicking your office just yet. I just wanted to let you know, though… If they ask me to shuffle over to Milton House afterwards, I'll tell them where to stick it.'

'You can't do that. You've got to do what's best for you.'

'I know. That's the whole point. This is best for me.

And anyway, you're the one who said you'd be left short if I wasn't around.'

Jack snorted. 'Yeah. Well, we can't have your head swelling up too much, can we?'

'Sure I can't tempt you with a quick pint?'

Jack shook his head. 'Nah. I'm sure. In any case, I need to get back for the girls.'

55

Jack carried the car seat awkwardly into the hospital, wondering how on earth he was going to manage to lift it or manoeuvre it with the additional weight of a baby. He guessed one benefit was that she didn't weigh very much at the moment, although he knew from experience how quickly that changed.

The doctors had made it clear they should watch her weight very carefully. Although she'd thrived in the neonatal intensive care unit and they'd finally got the all-clear to take her home, the outside world was a different thing entirely, and the change of environment could cause untold stresses to such a small, delicate body.

All in all, it would be a good day. The news that they were being discharged came just moments after Clive Blake had pleaded guilty at the dock. Sentencing was still to be decided, and he'd likely get a form of reduced sentence for pleading guilty at the earliest opportunity, but he still wouldn't be seeing the outside world for quite some time.

It felt fitting to Jack that Clive Blake was committed to incarceration on the same day his first grandchild was finally allowed out into society. The relevance wasn't lost on Jack that those two events had occurred not long after Frank's funeral and the closure of that particular chapter. But, try as he might, Jack considered it not so much a closed chapter, as a bookmarked one, the corner of the page folded over as a reminder that all was not quite over.

The multi-faceted betrayal he'd suffered at the hands of Helen and Gary McCann still cut deep, and it was one he knew was going to be rubbed in his face over and over. But it had merely bled into the background noise after everything else that'd happened over the past weeks. For now, he wasn't going to give them the mental space or energy to bother him. That would come. He knew it would. He wasn't naive enough to think otherwise. But it could wait. For now, he had other priorities.

'We all set?' he asked as he stepped into the room where Emily and Chrissie had been preparing to leave. 'Feels sort of like moving house, after the amount of time we've spent in here. I think I know these walls better than I know my own.'

'Well I dunno about you,' Emily said, 'but I won't miss them. I just can't wait for us all to be together in the one place, so we can actually get on with our lives again.'

Jack thought back to that night at McCann's house, discovering he'd not only tracked down Helen, but had sweet-talked her and moved her into his house. In a way, it gave him a small frisson of pleasure. They were the worst possible people for each other. Helen was desperate, keen to grab any attention she could. If anything, she was potentially the one person who could destroy McCann. She'd certainly done more than enough to Jack over the years. And, when McCann'd had enough of her, Jack knew Helen wouldn't just silently move out and move on. She had to make a drama out of everything. And McCann had form when it came to missing exes.

'Yeah,' he said, remembering Emily's comment. 'Yeah. We can get on with our lives.' He knew he'd have to tell her where Helen was. Emily was aware her mum was around Mildenheath, but she hadn't received any further contact since telling her to keep her distance. Jack had been surprised she'd taken heed of that request — for now, at least. But if there was one thing he knew about Helen, it was that she didn't stay quiet for long.

'Do you think we should tell her?' Emily asked, as if reading Jack's mind.

'Well, I guess that's up to you,' he replied, after a sharp intake of breath. 'I mean, she's got a right to know.'

'You think?'

'Don't you?'

'Not particularly. I think she gave up her rights the moment she walked out on you. On us. As far as I'm concerned, I've got my family now. Just the four of us.'

Jack looked at Chrissie and smiled. He certainly couldn't argue with that.

．　．　．

A short while later, once all the formalities had been completed, they emerged into the car park, where Jack had managed to nab a spot as close to the hospital as he could manage.

He opened the car door and secured Mia's carry seat onto its base. 'Blimey. Been a while since I did this,' he said. 'And we didn't have all this fancy nonsense, either. I'm pretty sure we used to just strap you to the roof rack with a bungee cord.'

'Yeah yeah,' Emily said, trying not to reveal she'd actually found one of her dad's jokes funny. 'I can tell you've been practising, don't you worry.'

Jack stood up, admired his accomplishment and shrugged. 'Well, got to get it right, haven't you? I don't fancy doing an emergency stop and having this bloody great thing come crashing into the back of my head. Knackered my back up enough as it is, just carrying it here.'

'All ready?' Chrissie asked, as she got into the passenger seat.

'Think so,' Emily replied, looking down at her daughter. 'Ready as we'll ever be, anyway.'

Jack started the car and gently reversed it out of the parking bay. It was often said that the most careful car journey anyone ever takes is the first one with a newborn baby in the back, and he certainly wasn't about to break that tradition.

. . .

Helen pushed her sunglasses a little further up her nose and sank down in her seat, keen not to be spotted. She watched as Jack and his perfect little family pulled out onto the main road and headed for home.

When was he planning on telling her? Did he really think she was that stupid? Did he seriously believe she hadn't been keeping a very close eye on them all?

It hurt. The pain ran deep. And she was going to damn well make sure he knew it.

ACKNOWLEDGMENTS

When I realised late in 2020 that 5 January 2021 was the tenth anniversary of my very first book, *Too Close for Comfort*, I had a bit of a panic attack.

I like it when things fit together nicely, and it seemed only right that the tenth book in the Knight & Culverhouse series should be released on the tenth anniversary of the first. However, that left me more than a little tight for time.

It's taken some long days (and even longer nights) but I got there in the end. It's my assumption you've already read the book and haven't just skipped to this bit (if that's exactly what you've done, I'm doing my stern voice now and I suggest you close the book and start from the beginning, or I won't be very happy). Seeing as you've got this far, I'm hoping I've actually managed to pull it off.

It would be fair to say the Knight & Culverhouse series has taken on a life of its own. Each book takes the series in a completely new direction to what I'd intended or imagined, and I find it extraordinary how much the fictional world of Mildenheath has grown.

It's often difficult to keep exploring those same complexities without pumping out 500,000 word epics each time, but I'm quite enjoying the leaving-and-revisiting aspect of different characters' lives throughout the series, as and when the storyline demands their focus. In that way, I tend to think of the subplots of the characters' lives as being similar in structure to a soap opera. The storyline pulls the focus towards certain characters at different times.

That's something I really enjoy about writing this series. After ten years and ten books, there's a rich world already there in Mildenheath, and it's great fun to be able to revisit aspects and build on them as the series progresses.

But none of that would be possible without the assistance of some wonderful people who make sure I get my facts right (or at least let me know what the facts are so I can ignore them) and who help make my books the best they possibly can be.

My thanks, as always, go to Graham Bartlett. Having spent his life as a very high-ranking detective, he's invaluable in helping me navigate my way through police procedure, which is not only just as confusing after ten years as it was after ten minutes, but also constantly changing between books, seemingly just to annoy me.

Huge thanks also go to my wife, Jo, for reading the first drafts of everything I write, and either making sure it's not shit or making it less shit with her suggestions.

To Lucy, for her wonderful editing, eagle-eye and uncanny ability to make every one of my books a whole level better with her suggestions.

To my mum, who reads early versions of each book and helps make it less rubbish with ideas for improvements. Let's call this year's one your Christmas present.

To my son, James, for mostly keeping out of my office when I'm trying to write and NO I DON'T WANT TO PLAY PAW PATROL RIGHT NOW, I'M BUSY.

There are, I'm sure, dozens of other people I really need to thank, but it's Sunday evening, I had five hours' sleep and apparently I need to go and play Paw Patrol. Sorry to all of you. I really do appreciate your help, whoever you are.

A SPECIAL THANK YOU TO MY PATRONS

Thank you to everyone who's a member of my Patreon program. Active supporters get a number of benefits, including the chance of having a character named after them in my books. In *Snakes and Ladders*, Lisa Lewkowicz and Claire Evans were named after Patreon supporters.

With that, I'd like to give my biggest thanks to my small but growing group of readers who are currently signed up as Patreon supporters at the time of writing: Alexier Mayes, Anne Davies, Ann Sidey, Barbara Tallis, Carla Powell, Cheryl Hill, Claire Evans, Darren Ashworth, Dawn Blythe, Dawn Godsall, Di Norwood, Emiliana Anna Perrone, Estelle Golding, Geraldine Rue, Helen Brown, Helen Weir, Jeanette Moss, Josephine Graham, Judy Hopkins, Julie Devonald Cornelius, Karina Gallagher, Kerry Robb, Kirstin Anya Wallace, Leigh Hansen, Linda Anderson, Lisa Bayliss, Lisa Lewkowicz, Lisa-marie Thompson, Liz Kentish, Lynne Davis, Lynne Lester-George, Mandy Davies, Maureen Hutchings, Nigel

M Gibbs, Paul Wardle, Paula Holland, Peter Tottman, Ruralbob, Sally Catling, Sally-Anne Coton, Samantha Harris, Sim Croft, Sue, Susan Bingham, Susan Fiddes, Sylvia Crampin, Tracey Clark and Tremayne Alflatt. You're all absolute superstars.

If you're interested in becoming a patron, please head over to patreon.com/adamcroft. Your support is enormously valuable.

MORE BOOKS BY ADAM CROFT

RUTLAND CRIME SERIES

1. What Lies Beneath
2. On Borrowed Time
3. In Cold Blood

KNIGHT & CULVERHOUSE CRIME THRILLERS

1. Too Close for Comfort
2. Guilty as Sin
3. Jack Be Nimble
4. Rough Justice
5. In Too Deep
6. In The Name of the Father
7. With A Vengeance
8. Dead & Buried
9. In Too Deep
10. Snakes & Ladders

PSYCHOLOGICAL THRILLERS

- Her Last Tomorrow
- Only The Truth

- In Her Image
- Tell Me I'm Wrong
- The Perfect Lie
- Closer To You

KEMPSTON HARDWICK MYSTERIES

1. Exit Stage Left
2. The Westerlea House Mystery
3. Death Under the Sun
4. The Thirteenth Room
5. The Wrong Man

All titles are available to order from all good book shops.

Signed and personalised books available at adamcroft.net/shop

EBOOK-ONLY SHORT STORIES

- Gone
- The Harder They Fall
- Love You To Death
- The Defender

To find out more, visit adamcroft.net

GET MORE OF MY BOOKS FREE!

Thank you for reading *Snakes & Ladders*. I hope it was as much fun for you as it was for me writing it.

To say thank you, I'd like to give you some of my books and short stories for FREE. Read on to get yours...

If you enjoyed the book, please do leave a review online. Reviews mean an awful lot to writers and they help us to find new readers more than almost anything else. It would be very much appreciated.

I love hearing from my readers, too, so please do feel free to get in touch with me. You can contact me via my website, on Twitter @adamcroft and you can join my Facebook Readers Group at http://www.facebook.com/groups/adamcroft.

Last of all, but certainly not least, I'd like to let you know that members of my email club have access to FREE, exclusive books and short stories which aren't available anywhere else. There's a whole lot more, too, so please join the club (for free!) at https://www.adamcroft.net/vip-club

For more information, visit my website: adamcroft.net